His Taste of Christmas

P.S. Black

HIS TASTE OF CHRISTMAS

Edits: Sarah @ The Word Emporium

Cover Design: Temptation Creations

Formatting: PS. Black

Proofreader: Claire Buckley

ISBN: 978-1-916536-03-6

Playlist

Ashanti – Baby
Beyoncé – Speechless
Anne-Marie – Think Of Christmas
Willie Nelson, Norah Jones – Baby It's Cold Outside
Ariana Grande, Liz Gillies – Santa Baby
Two Feet – I Feel Like I'm Drowning
Mellina Tey – Watching Me
Muni Long – Hrs & Hrs
SMV – Weak
Gallant – Open Up
Trey Songz – Slow Motion
6LACK, Jhené Aiko – First Fuck

Trigger list

Please see below trigger list, and please also know this is based in the UK, all ages are legal. :

Large age gap (22 years)

Power Dynamics

Relationship Dynamics (Possessiveness/Obsession)

Power Play

Use of food during sex

Dedication

To the people who, after reading this, won't be able to look at a candy cane without smiling... and thinking about Carter Hayes, of course.

Chapter One

Angel

"*It's beginning to look a lot like Christ—*"

"Hey! I was listening to that," Macey shouts, glaring at me from across the bar.

Rolling my eyes, I leave the counter and make my way to the tables to help her get ready for opening. I'm sick of listening to Macey's bloody Christmas songs. "It's bad enough that I have to listen to that crap every fucking day while living with you. I refuse to do it at work, Mace," I complain as I lower the chairs from a table.

"Ale—"

"Don't you fucking dare. If I hear one more Michael or Mariah song from that speaker, I will stamp out that Alexa." With narrowed eyes, I observe Macey, who smirks at me, appearing eager to challenge my threat. I raise an eyebrow and place a hand on my hip, silently challenging her to test me.

With a sickly sweet tone, she calls out, "Alexa, play..." She drags her instruction out and then in a jumbled rush of words, she shouts, "Christmas Hits playlist on Spotify."

I spin on my heels and stalk towards the Alexa. As the speaker starts playing yet another stupid Christmas song, Macey's laughter fills the room. Of course, I'm not entirely crazy. I wouldn't destroy the speaker simply because it plays Christmas songs. Well, not on a day when I'm in an okay mood, anyway.

With her boots slapping and echoing through the room, Macey hurries in my direction, screeching "Angel" from behind me.

With a grin, I start running too, but I don't get far. Macey tackles me from behind, resulting in a loud scream leaving my mouth and both of us tumbling to the floor, followed by fits of laughter.

Macey has been my best friend since I can remember. During our childhood, we lived next door and were inseparable, attending school together. We both got accepted into a college in Chelsea. Their literature program is top-notch, which is great for me since I love writing, and Mace has always had a passion for business finance. The moment we learned about the college's programs for both of us, we made up our minds to stay together and not look elsewhere.

We lived in South London with our parents, which we adored, but the daily commute was pure torture. We would often be out for more than fourteen hours, returning home only to eat, shower, and crash into bed, ready to repeat the process the next day. We were walking zombies.

It was only by some stroke of luck—and much persuasion from my dad—that we were able to move into the flat above my parent's pub, on the condition that we help out behind the bar when needed. Given our upbringing in this place and early experience pouring pints, it was a clear choice.

This pub has been in my family for centuries, and with it looking over London Bridge, it's much closer to the college. It's a trendy pub that is always busy. This year, though, Mace and I are pissed about the work situation. My parents are going on holiday, so we have to run the place throughout the Christmas period, and that includes being open on Christmas Day. So now Mace and I are stuck here, managing this place during the busiest time of the year. The problem isn't managing the pub. It's the bloody festive people that do me in.

Mace being one of them.

"Girls!"

I roll off Macey at the sound of the stern shout, flicking my gaze to meet my dad's emerald-green eyes. His expression is sour at the sight of Macey and I on the floor. "I have a feeling that it's a big mistake to leave you two in charge while your mum and I go away."

Leaping up onto my feet, I brush my hands against my thighs, wiping away the dust. "Dad. Come on. You know we can do this. We'll be fine."

His eyes fall to Mace, who is still lying on the floor as she smiles up at him. "Kane, I can assure you that I won't cause any issues. It's your daughter who'll lead you to bankruptcy." He extends his hand to Mace, who takes hold of it to help her stand. Then she motions to me. "This Miss Grinch will frighten away all the customers. She won't even let me play Christmas songs." She rolls her eyes. "It's bloody Christmas, Kane. Sort her out." Casting a smirk my way, she lets me know she's won. Christmas is adored by my dad and, in fact, my entire family.

"Angel face."

My dad's eyes land on me while Mace mumbles, "More like witch face." Just as I flash a fake smile and flip her off, my dad comes over and surprises me with a warm hug.

"I understand that you're not very festive, but please try to be while your mum and I are away. Do you think you can do that?"

I lean in and place my head against his chest, nodding. "Sure thing, Dad. Don't stress. Everything is going to be fine." I step back and flash him a reassuring smile.

"Kane," Mace says with a mischievous glint in her eyes. "What's the reason behind Angel's strong dislike for Christmas? I'm guessing it's unresolved trauma from the year you and Krystal didn't purchase the Barbie Dream House for her."

"Watch me spit in your tea tomorrow morning."

"Girls," Dad deadpans. "Stop winding each other up."

Chapter Two

Angel

"Okay. Angel, are you certain that you both will be okay?" Mum asks for the fourth time today.

I sigh as I place my groceries on the kitchen countertop and then swiftly spin to face her. I grasp her hands, noticing the way her shoulders slump and her brows furrow. With a small smile, I tilt my head to the side. I know what she wants me to say. 'Please don't go to Ireland. Stay here for Christmas with me'. She's searching for any excuse not to go, but my dad has put his foot down and said they will spend Christmas with his family this year.

I wish I had the time to join them, but while I'll miss my family, I still need to finish a writing project by the start of term in the New Year, which I haven't even started. Mum thinks running the pub will distract me from focusing on it, but it's just a short story, and I keep reassuring her I'll have enough time. I wouldn't give it a second thought if I went to Ireland with them and I need to do well so I can get a place at university.

"Mum..." I stretch out the word, clutching her hand while bringing her closer to me, and wrap one arm around her shoulder before burying my face in her hair. I hear her mumbling, so I pull away slightly. "What?" I ask. Her wide, green eyes, mirroring my own, hold my gaze as she lifts her hand and lovingly runs her fingers through my dark-brown locks.

"You're Miss Grinch at the best of times. How can I trust that you will actually celebrate Christmas when we're not here?"

A sigh escapes me as I roll my eyes. "Firstly, Mother, I share a home with someone who is obsessed with all things Christmas. Secondly, we'll be working behind the bar on Christmas Day so I can't just ignore it, can I? Happy Christmas to me," I exclaim sarcastically, pumping my fists in the air. "Stop worrying. I'll be fine, and *you* will be pleased to know that Mace and I are going Christmas decoration shopping tomorrow to decorate the pub. I'll be surprised if Mace can manage to get any sleep tonight. She hasn't stopped talking about it."

Giggling, she leans forward and plants a tender kiss on my forehead. "I know how joyless this is going to be for you." She smiles sympathetically as she pulls back. "And I appreciate it."

"Anything for you, Mum." I give her a final squeeze before turning to leave, glancing back over my shoulder. "I'm going to head upstairs and make a start on this story."

"Alright, hunny. I'll be heading out soon, but your dad and I will be back tomorrow to wrap up a few loose ends before we leave."

"Okay, Mum. Night. Love you." I exit the pub from the back and climb the stairs to our cosy flat. With hesitation, I open the door and listen, exhaling in relief that I can't hear *Michael Bublé* blasting from the speakers.

"Mace," I call as I enter the hallway, quickly scanning the small space.

She wasn't in the pub when I was talking to Mum, but I didn't see her leave either. I thought she came up here to rest before our shift, but the lack of music playing isn't normal for her. As I enter the living room, I spot the six-foot Christmas tree that overwhelms our small space. There is not a single flickering light on the branches. Thank God.

"I'm in here!" Macey calls from her bedroom. Wearing a frown, I approach it and glance through the tiny gap in her slightly open door, unsure of what I will come face to face with. It's completely different from what I anticipated. Macey never studies silently. She always has a film or music on. Macey doesn't do silent.

"What's wrong?" I search her room for a clue about why she's studying silently. "Do I need to ring your mum?"

Her lips curl into a smirk as she looks up at me and says, "I've just been speaking with Tay. She mentioned the topic for your project assignment you have to do over the holiday has been sent.." Her smile grows wide. "Have you seen your emails?"

A wave of anxiety settles in my stomach as my brow furrows. It can't be anything too bad, but I know what that smile of Macey's means. I already know that I'm going to hate whatever is in my inbox.

I trail after her into my bedroom, where she grabs my laptop and positions herself against my bed. Opening the lid brings the screen to life, illuminating her lingering evil smile. Her gaze darts across the screen, and I could have sworn I detected a glimmer of excitement in her eyes. I inwardly groan. This is surely a bad sign. Closing the distance, I cautiously come up beside her and look down at the laptop screen to see that she has opened my emails.

"Here." Excitement fills her high-pitched voice as she hands the laptop over to me.

Instantly I notice an email from my teacher with the heading: 'Assignment subject'. We were told we had to write about a specific topic but not given any details other than the instructions would be sent to us during the holidays.

Mace's excitement confuses me, so I scroll down, trying to find out more.

Dear class,

I hope all is well and you're all ready for Christmas.

Your short story assignment subject for the holiday is 'Christmas cheer.' The short story can be no more than 15,000 words. I'm happy for you to write a story using your own personal experiences of what makes you happy at Christmas, but I'm also happy for you to fictionalise the story.

I look forward to reading your stories in the New Year.

I hope you all have a fantastic Christmas and a Happy New Year.

Kindest regards,

Miss Cody.

"Why do they never go for something unique" I groan, setting my laptop on the bed, although deep down I want to throw it to the floor. Plunging headfirst into my duvet, I let out a scream, then sigh as I roll over. "Seriously, why choose something so cliché?" I prop myself up on my arms, and Macey mirrors my body, her face just centimetres from mine, looking smug.

"Angel, it's time for you to start embracing the Christmas spirit."

I use my hand to cover her face and push her away playfully. "Go play with traffic, you nasty girl." I show her my middle finger. “How can you be this joyful, knowing the impact this has on my grade, you bitch?”

“Suck it up, buttercup,” she sings songs, pushing up off the bed before she skips out of the room and the words “Alexa, play Christmas songs” reach my ears.

I'm strangely drawn to the idea of murder at this moment.

Chapter Three

Angel

"Mace, you're going a little overboard, don't you think? We really don't need *all* these decorations." I glance at the colossal warehouse trolley she pushes in front of her. If she adds a couple more boxes to that stack, she won't be able to see over it. It is overloaded with nearly every Christmas decoration in here. My dad handed us his Costco card and told us to fully stock and decorate the pub. Mace, annoyingly, took his words literally and went running.

Much to my displeasure, I am now involved in helping her with the decoration purchases. I couldn't leave her alone to do it; despite my prayers that she would tell me to wait outside or go get a coffee while she shopped. She believes this will spark some inspiration in me for my project assignment.

She's wrong.

At the moment, all I'm inspired to do is hope that something large and heavy falls from a top shelf and flattens me like a pancake.

"Omg! We have to get this," I cry.

"Oh, what is it?" Macey walks to where I've stopped. I see a flicker of excitement in her eyes, which I can only assume is due to me finally mentioning a purchase, but then she hisses, "No chance, you freak," before storming back to her abandoned cart.

"It would be unconventional, but I think it would make the pub stand out."

As she turns, her hand finds its place on her hip, and her brow lifts. "Putting a Christmas hat on Ghostface won't attract people to the pub. They'll think it's some emo shack with people popping pills."

I chuckle quietly to myself. I find pleasure in getting a rise out of her. She shakes her head and guides the trolley down the aisle until she comes to a halt in front of a ten-foot inflatable Father Christmas.

"Oh. My. God!" she shrieks.

I increase my speed to catch up with her. "Absolutely fucking not. No. No. And NO!" I make it clear that we are not going home with this.

She waves her hand at me and takes out her phone. "Shh." After capturing an image of the item in question, she furiously taps on the screen. I stealthily move closer to her and glance over her shoulder.

"What are you..." I gasp. "You're asking my dad. You sneaky little bitch."

I receive no response as she persistently taps away on her phone. While she waits for a reply, she stares up at Father Christmas with a mesmerised expression on her face, as if she has already decided exactly where it will go. Her phone pings and she glances at the screen.

"Kane thinks it's great but says it won't work outside the pub because we won't have anywhere to tie it." With a pouting expression and a wrinkled nose, she strolls down the aisle, resembling a child about to have a tantrum.

Praise the heavens that Dad had some sense.

I shoot Father Christmas one last disgusted look before trailing after her.

I observe the customers around us and notice how joyful they all seem. *Why don't people act like this all year long? Why do presents and decorations have the power to make everyone happy?*

Christmas has always irritated me for this exact reason. It seems artificial and excessively exaggerated. People often pretend to be happy even if they're not and they waste an absurd amount of money. I wouldn't necessarily use the word 'hate' to describe my feelings towards Christmas, but it's all too much. And this year, I have to spend it with Mace, so I think it will be worse than ever.

My eyes keep scanning the shop floor, taking in the abundance of red and the combination of green, gold and silver, which is irritatingly beautiful.

I let out a grunt of pain as I collide with a solid object. As I raise my eyes, I come face to face with a broad back that is double my size. I stare at the taut white shirt, on the verge of tearing from being stretched across the clearly defined rippling muscles. My gaze continues, eventually fixating on his dishevelled yet stylishly arranged brown hair. I'm hit with the need to feel it with my fingers.

Without warning, a meticulously maintained stubble catches my eye, before dark hazel eyes capture me. It feels like time slows down when he looks at me. He squints, and little lines appear around his eyes, making my stomach tighten. His smile is bright and his teeth sparkle. I can't look away. This all looks too familiar.

Am I currently dreaming? Could this be a figment of my imagination?

A frown appears on his beautiful face, causing the laughter lines around his eyes to become less prominent. I realise I'll do anything to get that smile back.

He moves closer, standing tall above me. Wow, he's massive. He must be at least 6 ft 5.

"Angel?" The screech of my name resonates in my ear. I briefly close my stinging eyes that were open and unblinking for too long and refocus.

This is not a dream. I'm still, in fact, in Costco, but that beautiful smile is now back and those gorgeous eyes are still there, and holy shit...

"Snap out of it. What's the matter with you?" Macey's eyes are wide when I finally turn my attention back to her. "I'm sorry, Mr Hayes. I don't know what's wrong with her."

Wait, did she really say Mr Hayes?

My stomach sinks.

She did. She did because Mr Hayes is currently standing in front of me.

The man who stirred butterflies in my stomach during school lessons. The man who ignited a fire in me every time he spoke—the man who created my passion for writing. I've been standing here, completely fixated, as my old English teacher stands right in front of me.

Fantastic.

Fabulous.

Fuck!

"Uh, I'm, uh..." I lower my head, my gaze fixed on the ground, praying for it to open up and consume me entirely. I never learned how to talk to him without blushing, and now that I'm near him, my cheeks feel like they're on fire. Being around him is apparently still too much for my body to handle because there's a familiar stirring in my stomach.

"Angel?" His voice, rough and deep, sends signals to my core between my thighs, leaving behind a deep ache that I thought had long vanished.

I wince as there's a sharp jab to my side. Mace is likely just as embarrassed as me about my behaviour. In school, she thought it was hilarious, but now we're both eighteen, this shouldn't be happening.

Raising my head, I inhale deeply. His eyes, like shards of auburn crystal, pierce through me, leaving me breathless. He has always been handsome, but now he's unbelievably captivating. The grey that now shines through his brown hair and the days-old stubble really, and I mean *really*, does it for him. He looks older, but in a good way. I have never found an older man with what is the start of grey hair attractive, but he just took the crown for that because, wow, just wow. I'm doing it again. *Shit.*

"Hi." *Hi? That is all I have after all of that. For fuck's sake.* "Sorry, Mr Hayes," I quickly rush out, desperately searching for an excuse for my probably obvious reaction to seeing him. "Late night, last night. I can't seem to stay focused." I grimace and briefly glance at him before turning my attention to Mace, who looks at me with a dumbfounded expression.

With a less-than-subtle gesture, she shakes her head, indicating that I need to handle and resolve this. I glance back at Mr Hayes, who wears a smirk, suggesting he is aware of why I'm so flustered. He must not be bothered by the fact that I was just checking him out. I guess he is no longer our teacher.

"Angel." He acknowledges me with a nod, his smirk transforming back into that wide grin I love so much. The ache between my thighs intensifies once again. Fuck, I need to get laid to get rid of this feeling, but who am I kidding? I've never got laid. Thinking about him is the only time I experience this feeling. Thoughts of him cross my mind while I am in bed and my fingers creep beneath my sleep shorts, or when I'm showering and decide to use the shower head between my legs. I can only reach orgasm when I visualise him.

As I try to shake off my frustration, Mr Hayes raises an eyebrow.

"Are you zoning out again?" A smirk plays on his lips while his eyes twinkle. He's definitely messing with me.

"I guess I'm a lot more tired than I thought." I give him a restrained smile, hoping Mace will catch on and find a way to get us out of this situation. Despite my efforts, she continues to ignore me and focuses her attention solely on Mr Hayes.

"Merry Christmas, Mr Hayes," Mace says way too cheerfully, her grin so wide her eyes squint into tiny slits.

He extends his hand. "Please, Macey, we're not in school anymore. Call me Carter," he informs her. "Merry Christmas to you both." I meet his gaze and try to hide my nervousness, swallowing to combat the dryness in my throat, hoping he doesn't notice my blushing face. I must blend in with all the red decorations in this shop.

"You got any plans this Christmas, Carter?" Mace asks, his name so casual on her tongue. Calling him that would feel too casual for me. I can hardly even make eye contact with the man, let alone be familiar enough to call him by his first name.

"None at the moment. I'm here to restock on cases of wine and beers and some Christmas stuff for my mum." He gestures towards his trolley, which is much smaller than the one Mace is pushing. He diverts his attention to Mace's trolley.

"It seems like you ladies are putting a lot of effort in this Christmas. What plans do you have?" With his gaze shifting between Mace and me. I keep quiet, trusting my bestie to do what she does best and direct the conversation.

"Oh, Angel's parents run a pub, and we're stuck managing it while they're away. Makes sense since we live upstairs. We're on the hunt for decorations today. Since we're open on Christmas Day, we should make it as festive and enjoyable as we can. I want it to feel like home from home for everyone who has booked, but just with them being waited on instead of having to do it themselves." Mace's wide grin stretches across her face as she rocks back and forth from her toes to her heels. Mace's excitement is palpable.

I don't realise that I must be wearing my festive-hating feelings on my face until Mr Hayes turns to me and asks, "Are you not looking forward to working on Christmas?" My tongue feels swollen, but I can't embarrass myself any further by keeping quiet.

"It's not really about my work," I try to explain, but Mace cuts me off before I can say anything else.

"She has a strong hatred for Christmas." Squinting, I turn my gaze towards her. People's reaction are consistently dramatic upon discovering my disdain for the holiday. Was it necessary for her to tell Mr Hayes?

With a twitch of his mouth and raised eyebrows, he signals for me to continue.

"Christmas isn't really my thing, that's all." I roll my eyes. "Seriously," I wave my hand dismissively, "it's excessive and just another way for people to go broke." Beside me, I can hear a loud yawn and witness Mace theatrically fanning her hand against her mouth. "*Yes*, I know what you think, Mace." I poke her in the side, causing her to squeal and quickly move away from me. Mr Hayes appears to be trying to suppress his smile as he watches our playful interaction.

"Is there anything you find appealing about Christmas?" he questions in an unbothered manner, free from judgment. Just asking out of curiosity, I suppose. Despite my shy smile, I can't resist sharing what's on my mind, even after eating a whole box today.

"Candy canes." I grin.

He brushes his thumb across his bottom lip slowly, and my eyes can't help but track every small movement he makes. I wonder what his lips feel like. I glance up and his eyes are fixed on me before he chuckles and gives a slow nod. "I wasn't expecting candy canes, but I get it; they are delicious."

With a smug grin, I direct my gaze at Mace. According to her, they taste awful and resemble toothpaste.

Mimicking her earlier words, I deadpan, "Mace has a strong hatred for candy canes." Once more, Mr Hayes chuckles and then grabs onto the handles of his trolley.

"I enjoyed seeing you both, but I have to go." He smiles and the moment of feeling normal around him washes away quickly, the wave of awkwardness drowning me again. I give him a shy finger wave and a closed-mouth smile.

"Bye, Mr Hayes."

"Bye, Carter," Mace shouts louder than she needs to be. "I hope you have a wonderful, jolly Christmas." Spinning on her heels, she giggles while turning her attention to more decorations. I lower my chin and start to walk away, but then there is the gentle touch of fingers on my sleeve, grazing my arm. My head pops up and my eyes land on Mr Hayes. His fingers move to dance over the sliver of skin exposed on my wrist.

"I forgot to ask," he says quietly, his eyes bouncing between mine. "What is the name of your parents' pub?"

My breathing falters. Oh God. Don't tell me he is going to turn up one day. One side of me doesn't want him to, but then there's a part of me that would do just about anything to see him again.

“Uh ... it’s called The Black Rose.”

“The Black Rose.” His whispered words remain suspended in the air as his breath gently caresses my cheeks. I’m not sure when, but he seems to have got closer to me. I remain in place. My gaze fixed on him. The scent of his aftershave is so captivating, I would willingly bathe in it. *Is it considered creepy if I move closer and take a quick sniff of him? No, yes, that would be weird. Stop.*

“Pretty name.” His gaze sweeps across my face, and his attention takes my breath away. I think I've completely forgotten the art of breathing. We stand in silence, our eyes locked in a heated stare that stretches on for what feels like a never-ending minute. I'm startled by a distant crash, causing me to break the connection. He steps away from me, and I dramatically release the breath I had been holding in my throat. Once again, he clutches his shopping cart, a small smile appearing as he murmurs, “See you around, Angel.” Without looking back, he walks away, leaving me stunned.

What the fuck just happened? Did I create all of that in my mind? Was that the start of my fantasies taking over my brain with how he looked at me?

Chapter Four

Carter

Even after I've walked away, her sweet lingering scent remains for at least five minutes. There's no denying that Angel O'Sullivan has matured over the past two years. Teachers claim they don't have favourite students, but that's bullshit. Angel was always mine. In the early years of her schooling, she was much more talkative with me. Her refreshing honesty and unique perspective on life intrigued me. I used to look forward to her creative writing tests. Her stories were captivating, even to me. I would get lost in them, and that was coming from a thirteen-year-old girl. She would create these worlds that would take you on a ride. Without fail, she was my star student every single year.

There was a significant transformation in her when she entered her last year of school. Boys tend to remain immature, but girls seem to become entirely different individuals by Year Eleven. It was a different kind of experience for Angel. Of course it was, because there's no one quite like Angel.

Rather than focusing on make-up and boys, she became silent. I'm not sure what caused it, but she started speaking less. To me, at least.

Every time I got close to her, she became restless or timid. It wasn't like her at all. I expressed my concerns to her Head of Year, and she told me, "She has a crush on you." Initially, I brushed it off, but gradually, I started noticing her strange behaviour. Whenever I glanced at her, she would abruptly turn her head as if she'd been looking at me. Her cheeks turned pink whenever we spoke, and she avoided me as much as she could.

Suddenly, Angel appeared in a different light. My eyes couldn't stray from the curves that seemed to emerge overnight. Her long, slender legs were more prominent thanks to the shorter skirt she wore—an unintentional torture. Every glance my way felt electric, her mere presence igniting a storm of conflicting emotions within me. My mouth would go like a desert as she would flip her hair to one side, revealing her delicate, slender neck. She had this thing where she would run her pen up and down the side of her neck whenever she was deep in concentration, and I hated how much I wished it were my lips instead. By now, I realised I had an attraction to Angel, and I was relieved to have only six months left before she finished her exams and left school, so I started distancing myself from her.

She was sixteen, for fuck's sake.

I was thirty-eight.

Was it legal? Yes, only just, but in every way, it was sickening; I was her teacher; she was twenty-two years younger than me.

She was my student, for crying out loud.

There were so many things wrong. Professionally, I was always intrigued by the girl, but my interest became all-consuming. My dreams were plagued by her night after night. I hated myself when I would wake up and be hard as a rock, and the only way to relieve myself was to fist myself to images of her. I hated the way my dick would strain my work pants when I would get just a whiff of her perfume when she walked by my desk. The way my eyes would gravitate to her lips every time she spoke, wishing I could feel how smooth they were against mine.

Her departure from school brought a sense of relief, as if I could finally breathe. Yet that feeling of relief quickly morphed into a longing. Longing to see her again, longing to speak with her. I missed her. I missed the stolen glances, her garnet-green eyes that sparkled like emeralds. I missed her so much that I was soon drowning in want and need.

I knew I couldn't have her, so I watched her from afar for the last two years, and it helped. Something in me eased by the sight of her. Even if the only way was through her social media posts. Then she was tagged in a picture with a boy. This was the first time I had seen Angel with a boy, and

I didn't like it one bit. My obsession grew into something intense at that point. I have never felt anger and jealousy as much as I did when I saw his arm hanging over her shoulder and both of them smiling broadly at the camera. I told myself it was to be expected, but all of a sudden looking at pictures of her on socials wasn't enough to satisfy my cravings for her. It felt like a switch flipped inside me when I saw her with a boy.

I wanted more.

I *needed* more.

So, I set things in motion—strategies for getting closer to her. I had a strong desire to see her in the flesh, but this newfound feeling was completely consuming, and I had an overwhelming hunger to touch and be with her all the time.

I saw on her socials that Macey had tagged her in a post saying how excited she was to go Christmas decoration shopping at Costco today. I knew this would be my moment. My thirst for her outweighed everything else. I needed to see her up close. Of course I had no idea what time they would be going there, so I parked on the street of their pub where, due to my social media stalking, I already knew she lived and I waited. I only caught a glimpse of her getting into a taxi, but even that tiny glimpse, and the knowledge that I would see her up close today, had me driving to Costco with a stomach full of butterflies.

Seeing and speaking to her just now has made me feel erratic, like I want to go and claim her in front of everyone in this store and tell them she's mine and always has been. *Fuck what is wrong with me?* I press my thumbs into my eyes to close them, but she is still all I see.

Her scent reached me before I could even face her. The scent of her school perfume has stayed the same; a scent I've only ever smelt on her. The sight of her made me lose my breath. My lungs burned as I stared at her. The fact she bumped into me feels like a sign this was the right move following her here today, a sign to say this was meant to be. I had to regain myself quickly before Macey noticed. Fortunately, Angel appeared equally stunned and simply stared at me without saying a word, her eyes drinking in my presence as if encountering me for the first time. In all honesty, seeing Angel today feels like the first time. Her pictures online don't do her justice. Her hips have filled out, which was clear in the tight leggings she was wearing. I noticed more than one man eye her from behind, which made me want to grab her and hide her from the world. Her large eyes followed my every move, overshadowed by lengthy black lashes that intensified their glistening green hue. Her wavy dark brown hair cascaded down her front, drawing attention to her perky tits that I instantly desired, imagining what they would look like in the flesh. My mind is consumed by the image of how fucking beautiful she would look bent over a desk with her hair tangled around my fist, as I thrust into her, hearing her bliss-filled cries. *Fuck*. My dick stirs at the thought. I knew if I got too close, this is what would happen. I zone back into what I'm meant to be doing and realise I have passed everything I need.

I knew my mum would be needing some more snacks for Christmas Day, so I told her I would get it while here today. Just like always, she asked the whole family to come over for Christmas. Eighteen of us. I love Christmas, but I have a big family, so you have no choice. When I was a kid, my house resembled Santa's Grotto.

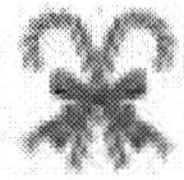

I'm at the checkout, queuing, and I can see Angel at another till with Macey. I can't take my eyes off her sexy as fuck figure. *Where did that peachy arse come from?* I have never seen her look so sexy before. I'm relieved that she hasn't noticed me, so I can keep watching her. I've convinced myself that I will go back to watching her from afar, but I know I won't be able to. My thirst for her is the strongest it's ever been and smelling her again has made it impossible to stay away. It's like her smell is imprinted on me now.

Two years ago, I was meant to forget about Angel O'Sullivan; she was my sixteen-year-old student.

Now?

She is an eighteen-year-old woman I have a serious obsession with that just keeps growing.

My eyes don't stray from her as she eye-rolls Macey for something I can't hear, while swirling a candy cane in her mouth, which makes me ponder what other things she could be doing with those plump lips.

I inwardly sigh with annoyance. *How am I going to get her out of my head?* As if she knows I'm watching, taunting and teasingly, she moves the candy cane in and out of her mouth. My sick and twisted mind imagines replacing it with my dick as she sucks me down, wondering how deeply she could take me.

My jeans become uncomfortably tight as my now hard cock presses against them. I shut my eyes and clench my teeth with more force than ever before. She's like a living fantasy come true. *Fuck my life.* I strain to open my eyes and when I do, everything freezes around me. Angel's gaze locks with mine as she lazily moves the candy cane in and out of her mouth, then she pulls it free, her mouth forming a small O.

"Sir?" I'm snapped out of my Angel-trance by a gentle voice. With a slight frown, a woman motions towards the now empty checkout. The cashier looks displeased, likely wondering why I'm causing a holdup. I quickly load my items onto the conveyor belt, wondering if anyone clocked who I was staring at. I really want to see her face again, but I have to go. I glance behind me as the cashier scans my items much faster than usual, likely annoyed, but Angel is not there, and the overwhelming disappointment serves as confirmation.

I need to breathe her in, to feel her presence consume me. The thought of her scent, her touch. It's driving me mad. I can't escape it. I can't escape her.

I need to smell her again.

I need to see her again.

Chapter Five

Angel

"Angel, are you even listening to me?" Mace whines while we unpack everything we bought at Costco, but I'm not listening to her as I can't get Mr Hayes out of my head. All I can picture are those unwavering eyes that trapped me.

"Angel O'Sullivan," she shrieks loudly, prompting me to scrub my hand down my face. I can't believe she spent six hundred pounds on decorations. Who does that? Of course, she went on about how my dad said this and my dad said that. He looks at Mace like another daughter, and I'm pretty sure he wishes she really was for Christmas. Both of them are equally obsessed with this time of year.

"Yes," I mutter. But I wasn't, just like I wasn't during the entire trip back from the store.

"What did I say then?" she snaps. As I glance up at her, she stands with her hands full of baubles and a raised eyebrow.

"How much you love the colour scheme you have gone with this year?"

Without hesitation, her raised eyebrow returns to its original position. "Oh, okay, my mistake. You were actually listening." Contently, she starts unpacking more decorations. I grin to myself while doing the same. I didn't hear a word that came out of her mouth, but being best friends since you were six-years-old pays off. I know this girl like the back of my hand.

"Your mum mentioned that the men will arrive tomorrow to set up the decorations, but I'm popping out with my mum. Are you free tomorrow?"

I nod my head, "Yes. I have a free day, so I'll be here. That's fine."

"Great, your mum said she could be here if not." Tomorrow is the day she leaves for Ireland. I don't expect her to be here dealing with that. "I'll text her later and let her know." It could be seen as strange that Macey is the one who arranges things with my parents more frequently than I do, but it's completely normal for us. She has been in the family since I can remember, and when it comes to Christmas, I would rather voluntarily pull every single strand of hair from my scalp than be left to deal with it, so I don't mind in the slightest that Mace does everything. We have a team of people who are hired to put up all the decorations, but Macey insists on decorating the tree in the pub.

Unfortunately, we already have one in our apartment, and it was set up on 1st November. Despite the limited room, she opted for the biggest one she could manage. Nevertheless, I firmly stated that the pub's tree wouldn't be put up until ten days prior to Christmas. I was persistent in my foot stomping, and I eventually got my way.

Naturally, we had to set up some decorations. We're running a pub. There have been customers who are genuinely thankful for our non-excessive setting. There are lots of them who believe the decorations shouldn't be set up too soon. I can't help but give Macey a smug smile whenever they agree with me.

Macey grabs the iPad and starts to review the pub's email account. Our Christmas Day bookings will close tomorrow to allow us two weeks for the preparations.

"Do we have any more bookings?" I ask her. Our reservations were almost full, with only two tables remaining. This is our most successful year yet. Another reason my parents had to be skeptical about going away. Despite their concerns, Mace and I have shown we can manage a busy pub. Our team is highly experienced and ready to provide plenty of assistance.

Our chef is what I like to call top-notch. I'm biased, but Harry does the best pub grub in London. I constantly tell him that he can be my live-in chef when I become rich. Although he does cook me dinners before closing up most nights, so he's basically already doing it.

“I'm currently checking, but it doesn't seem like it,” she says, while continuing to read.

“Alright, I'm going to take a shower and then attempt to begin this short story.”

Macey's giggles echo as I reluctantly make my way to the door. “I'm looking forward to seeing your work,” she sing songs.

I close my bedroom door with a bit too much force before I collapse onto my bed, turn on my laptop, and go through the project again. There are no strict guidelines, but it must be related to Christmas.

I open up a Word document and fixate on the empty white screen, longing for an idea to surprise me, but I am left disappointed. I'm at a loss for where to start. *What the hell am I going to do?* While I know Mace would be willing to help me come up with something, I need to handle this on my own. Going for a walk down Southbank might provide some relief, or perhaps I should just go to one of the Christmas markets and face it head-on. The fact I am lucky enough to have Covent Garden, Leicester Square, and even Winter Wonderland on my doorstep is just another reminder of how criminal it is I don’t like Christmas. Honestly, London City is the ultimate festive destination, and I'm right in the heart of it.

It's unfortunate for me.

"Damn it, I can't do this," I cry. I need to find inspiration, and that won't happen if I keep staring at a blank screen. What I really need right now is a hot and relaxing shower to rid myself of all my worries.

I strip down and walk into my en suite. I shamelessly used the line "it's my parents' pub" to justify why I deserve the only en suite bedroom in this flat. Mace was happy. She got the main bathroom to herself, which has a killer tub—one I use regularly.

As I turn on the shower and step inside, the room fills with steam. People often underestimate the calming effects of standing in a shower with a searing stream when feeling stressed. It completely removes any worries.

Standing in place, I let the water saturate my hair and cascade over me for a good five minutes. I'm loving the feeling of having a blank mind. Despite my efforts to focus on the calming effects of running water and its warmth on my muscles, the face of someone I can't shake off continues to intrude into my thoughts.

Goosebumps snake their way up my body, bringing back a familiar feeling. I tilt my head back, grateful for the strong water pressure. The forceful jets hit my nipples as I imagine his touch. The closer my hand gets to my centre, the faster my breathing becomes. Without wasting any time, I slip my fingers between my already wet folds. The swelling in my clit is making me crave his touch. It starts with one finger, then another one joins, both moving over the swollen bundle of nerves. I apply pressure and move my fingers in circular motions as the water beats against my body.

The ache starts in the pit of my stomach, a telltale sign that it won't be long before I'm falling over the edge. Increasing my speed, my body slumps against the cold tiled wall beside me, instantly cooling my overheated body, my breath catching.

I could watch you all day sucking on that candy cane, Angel. I picture Mr Hayes whispering in my ear as I pleasure myself for him. I imagine feeling his dick brushing against my arse cheeks, and the sudden thought of him bending me in half and burying himself in my tight hole flashes through my mind. I whimper. I have an insatiable hunger for him, and seeing him has only intensified that feeling.

I crave him.

Your tight, sweet arse is equally as beautiful as your big, juicy lips. Will you wash me when I finish spilling myself into your tight hole and then suck me dry? Angel, will you show your submission by getting on your knees for your daddy?

"Fuck," I mutter as I feel the orgasm coming in hard. It's right there—

"Oh, my fucking God!" My bathroom door flies open as Macey shouts, "Angel, get out of that shower now."

You have got to be kidding me. Mr Hayes disappears; every single thought and image evaporating from my head in a cloud of smoke. The orgasm that I was on the brink of disappears with a single snap. All because my best fucking friend chose now to burst into my bathroom, even though she can clearly hear the shower is on.

"Macey, what the fuck?" I seethe. Yes, Mace and I have that friendship where we sit on the toilet while another is in the bath. She's like my sister. We have seen everything there is to see of each other. But sometimes, just sometimes, I wish it wasn't like that with us.

"Angel Aoife O'Sullivan. You will not want to miss this information for a second longer. Get out here now." She hits the shower door forcefully. Fortunately, the mist on the glass obscures her vision entirely. I'm a little intrigued because she used my full name. She only uses that when she's really mad at me or has some mind-blowing gossip.

I turn off the shower, fully aware that I'll need to return, just so I can actually wash my hair and finally address the wetness between my legs, but I'm certain she won't leave until she reveals what's going on.

I step out of the shower; she is already standing there with a towel in her hand, and the smile on her face causes nerves to wash through me.

"Fuck, what's happened?" Macey skips out of my bathroom while I hastily wrap the towel around me. I follow her into my bedroom and find her standing next to my bed, grinning just like *Pennywise* does before he feasts on children's fear. "You're freaking me out. What's going on?" I question her, frowning.

"You won't believe it, but we just got a booking request for Christmas Day." Her grin, already big and creepy, becomes even more unsettling. "Great, please don't tell me this is why you are giving me *IT* vibes and dragged me out of the shower, Mace?" I lock eyes with her and shoot her a glare of pure frustration.

"It is," she replies matter-of-factly. My head leans back, and my eyebrows brush against my hairline.

"Were you brought into existence solely to infuriate me?" I stand, raising my hands and letting them slap against my thighs in disbelief. "What the fuck is your pro—"

"The reservation was made in the name of Carter Hayes."

Chapter Six

Carter

After making a request to book, I click the submit button. A request form needs to be filled out for bookings exceeding ten. I know it's weird, but I had to make a reservation at The Black Rose for Christmas dinner just to be near her again. I already knew the name of the pub. I've stood outside more times than I can count, willing myself to walk through the doors in the hope I would see her, but seeing her today felt like a sign, so I knew if I asked the name of the pub, my booking wouldn't come as a total surprise.

On the one hand, I'm considering visiting before Christmas, but on the other hand, I want to see her specifically on Christmas Day. I want to make her smile on the one day she doesn't feel like it.

Does she have a special outfit planned for Christmas Day? Is she going to be unhappy during Christmas? Is it possible for me to bring a smile to her face?

Sitting at the ripe age of forty, I'm constantly refreshing my phone as if I'm sixteen again waiting for the girl I like to text me. Tapping my foot anxiously, hoping for an acceptance from the pub. I considered going alone, but my mum wouldn't allow me to spend Christmas by myself. Despite telling her I was with friends, she would still insist on me bringing them along. Family is my mum's top priority, but Christmas comes in a close second. She loves it. I never expected her to agree to spend Christmas outside of the house. She's already prepared for dinner by ordering the turkey and buying all the frozen food, but I told her about this amazing pub that serves the best Christmas dinners and has great reviews. It took some persuading, but Mum agreed to go and got on the phone to the whole family.

I really hope it lives up to our expectations since we haven't gone out for Christmas in years. It would be a relief if neither she nor my aunts had to cook so they could enjoy the day with their family instead of slaving away in a hot kitchen. I suggested having finger food and turkey on Boxing Day, and I offered to help with it. She was surprisingly excited about doing something different. It's not your typical, run-of-the-mill pub in London either, it has character. Like it’s been passed down the generations. Everything in London is so modern looking and fancy. This place is cosy; it screams homely. A perfect place to be on Christmas Day.

I shared the pictures with Mum, and she absolutely loved them. I, of course have already seen the pub, but I haven’t been in there. I feel like shit for not telling Mum the real reason I want to go there. She would keel over if she found out it's because I want to see an eighteen-year-old girl. But to be honest, I don't care, age is just a number. My phone pings and I hastily glance at the screen, only to find it's a text message and not an email from the pub. It's my little brother.

Tyson:

Mum just told me we are at a pub in central for Christmas Day. Nice one. How did you sway that?

I chuckle to myself. My little brother, who is twenty-eight, is still in his 'wanting to sit in a pub every weekend' phase, so I knew when Mum agreed to this, there would at least be one person in the family over the moon with the idea.

Me:

Because I'm the favourite. I assumed you would have figured that out already.

It's far from the truth; Ty will always be Mum's golden child, but I like to wind him up sometimes.

Tyson:

In your dreams, old man.

I toss my phone onto the bed, hoping the rest of my family will be okay with my change of plan. My four brothers won't have any objections, I know. Although we're all easygoing, I'm unsure how my snooty aunties will handle being at a pub during Christmas. That is, if the booking is accepted. I entered my name in the hopes that it would make a difference, but if there's no availability, there's nothing to be done.

I still haven't figured out transportation. We're not far from Central London, but I don't want to inconvenience anyone, so I'll probably arrange for some taxis.

Relaxing on the sofa, I casually flip through the TV channels. Christmas is just ten days away, which means all the channels are filled with holiday classics. No matter what I watch on TV, I find myself unable to stop thinking about Angel and checking my phone. Texting her and asking if we have a table would be simpler, but I don't have her number. Suddenly, a thought pops into my head and I instinctively open Instagram. I feel like a stage ten creeper stalking her, but is it any better than booking in at her pub just to see her? I don't think so. I type 'An' in and her name pops up straight away. Of course it would. I check her profile weekly.

I find myself staring at one particular picture that I always gravitate to. She poses, but it's not sexual. Offering a small smile, the camera only reveals her exposed shoulders and her face. Although it's surprising for a young person to not be more in your face. I'm not surprised when it comes to Angel. She was always a good girl in school. Those eyes that tore through my soul only today, stare back at me.

I immediately picture her kneeling in front of me. Fuck. I wonder how many boys, if any, have seen her like that. I'm curious to know who she's let touch her.

My stomach stabs with pain at the mere thought. Fucking hell, what is wrong with me? This feeling shouldn't be here, but it is, and it has been for longer than I care to admit. I open up my direct messages and type out a message to her, but then think twice. I don't want to seem weirdly obsessed by searching her up on Instagram and messaging her. Even though I am.

I shut down my Instagram messages and place my phone on the sofa next to me. Resting my elbows on my knees, I tap my foot and rest my chin on my fists. I know you can wait days for a booking to be confirmed, but my mind won't stop racing and thinking of Angel. Image after image of her flashes through my mind, her beautiful eyes, her sexy as fuck lips. I need an excuse to see Angel again and this is the perfect one.

Fuck it.

I'm going to find out if my booking is accepted by walking right up to the bar and asking her myself.

Chapter Seven

Angel

"Can I have two Guinness, two Stellas, a rum and coke, and a vodka and coke, please?" a man at the bar orders.

"Coming right up," I respond before turning and sorting his order. It's busy tonight. It's a Friday, and a Friday in London for all the office workers means one thing: getting completely wasted and then crawling back home.

I have no complaints since we have a great group of customers who consistently fill our tills, which is excellent for business.

Mace is upstairs doing coursework, but if things get hectic, all I have to do is shout and I know she'll come and help.

I place the drinks in front of the gentleman, and he doesn't even wait for me to tell him how much before he hands me a few notes.

"Keep the change, love." I grin and give him an approving nod.

Our rush at the bar continues keeping me and the other bar staff busy. The place is filled with chatter, making it necessary for us to shout and lean over the bar to take orders.

Behind me, Laura shouts my name as I pour a pint. I steal a quick glance at her. Coming over, she raises her voice to shout in my ear. "There's someone over there who wants to talk to you." She gives a nod in the direction she wants me to look. I delay looking immediately because the pint I'm pouring fills up. I hand it over to the customer and quickly grab another glass to start pulling again as I glance behind Laura, but I don't see anyone familiar.

"Who?" I yell. Laura rotates and rises on her tiptoes, scanning her surroundings.

"He was right there," she says, glancing over the crowded bar, her eyes narrowing before widening with a small grin. "It was him." She indicates directly ahead of me. With a flick of my eyes, I'm rendered speechless as a familiar golden stare ignites my heartbeat and sends electric currents pulsing through me. The telltale signs of me not getting off earlier in the shower are all there as just one glance from Mr Hayes and the intense ache between my thighs returns instantly. With a slight nod, he gestures towards the side of the bar.

"Shit," I mutter as the pint I was pouring overflows, the beer spilling onto my hands. This doesn't faze me since I'm typically soaked in alcohol most evenings. The reason behind that happening is what matters. *What the fuck is he doing here?*

"Could you wrap up this order, Laura?" I shout. "It's just two Morettis."

She nods instantly, picking up a cloth. I head towards the side of the bar, lift the hatch to exit, and close it down. I turn on my heels, only to find Mr Hayes staring at me. I swiftly assess him. *Fuck my life.* He looks so hot in fitted jeans, trainers and a mid-length Parka coat. My core immediately concurs while my clit throbs.

"Hi, Mr Hayes." I try my utmost to plaster on a smile that says he doesn't affect me in any way, shape or form. "How can I help you?" I conceal my smile while he blatantly studies me. It feels like I'm being observed by the way he rakes his eyes over me.

"I haven't received any updates about the booking I made earlier today," he remarks, glancing at me and lingering on my black fishnet-covered legs. When our eyes meet again, he positions himself at the bar, crossing his feet and leaning on his elbow, like he's patiently awaiting my reply.

I can't explain why he has such a strong, intimidating effect on me. I become a bundle of nerves when he's around. When Mace told me earlier that he had booked in, she was confused, but, for some reason, so excited that he had.

According to her, her Christmas spirit attracts customers. I was going through an internal meltdown that she had no clue about. How on earth am I supposed to serve over a hundred people with him nearby? I find it challenging enough to take consecutive steps when he's present, and seeing him in Costco proved that his effect on me hasn't lessened with time.

My mind races as I think about the seventeen other people included in his booking. Are we talking about a girlfriend and her extended family? That can't be it, right? The thought of seeing him with another woman would shatter me. I discreetly checked his ring finger while we were in Costco and saw nothing, but that doesn't ease my anxiety.

"Um, yeah, well, Mace is the one responsible for handling that." My eyes quickly shift downwards towards my feet. Despite Mace's reservations about seating eighteen people, *Carter's* involvement gave her confidence in finding a solution. I, on the other hand, was finding every way to consider why it wouldn't work. Yes, I wanted to see him again, but I definitely didn't want it to be on Christmas Day—the worst day of the year.

I must stop acting so childishly around him, so I quickly lift my head and meet his gaze. With each passing second, my heart quickens.

"Look, I need to get back to work. I have no doubt that Mace will be in touch." He frowns a little, glancing behind me before a big smile appears.

"Mr Hayes," Mace says in a much louder volume than required, given that she's now standing next to us and this side of the bar is a lot quieter.

"Were your ears burning, Macey?" He laughs softly. "And, please, call me Carter." Well, that's odd. Not once has he given me permission to call him Carter. I observe his unwavering stare on Macey. When he looks at Macey, his eyes light up. *Oh my God, I bet he fancies her.*

"I'm going back to work," I inform Mace, squeezing past before I lose it in front of them both.

"I was just asking Angel about my reservation. She said you deal with those."

Laura comes to the hatch just as I'm about to lift it, determined to avoid hearing any more of Macey and Mr Hayes' conversation. "Ang," she interrupts, pulling my attention away, "could you please fetch some glasses? We're running pretty low."

I nod quickly, eager for the distraction, and manoeuvre past Macey and Mr Hayes. I make several trips back and forth, leaving the glasses at the bar for someone to load into the dishwasher. Each time I return, I glance around, hoping to see if Mr Hayes has gone.

When I look around again on my last trip, neither Mr Hayes nor Mace are anywhere to be seen. I assume he's gone and let out a heavy sigh of relief, only to be startled as someone suddenly appears in front of me, pushing me back.

In a busy pub, this isn't unusual, but the feel of fingers on the exposed skin of my waist is.

"Shit. Sorry, Angel." I look up to find Mr Hayes standing in front of me, his eyebrows knitted together in concern as he studies my face. "Are you okay?"

I nod, unable to find my voice, which seems to be a reoccurring effect around him. His fingers remain on my waist, touching the bare skin through the opening in my pinafore. His jaw tightens, and his expression becomes serious, as if he's just realized he's touching me.

I'm almost certain he moves closer to me, his presence becoming an overwhelming force as he stares down at me with an intensity that makes my pulse quicken. I meet his gaze, refusing to break eye contact, feeling a mix of defiance and anticipation. The pressure of his fingers tightening around my hips sends a shiver through my entire body, the sensation both thrilling and unnerving. Being this close to him makes my heart race, pounding furiously in my chest, each beat echoing in my ears. His head lowers slowly, and I become completely motionless, every muscle in my body tensing in anticipation. *Oh my God, is he about to kiss me? Is he really going to kiss me in front of this crowded pub?* The thought sends a rush of adrenaline through me.

He inches closer, his breath warm and tantalizing against my skin. Just when I think he's about to press his mouth to mine, he turns his head, and his lips graze my ear. The sensation is electric, sending a jolt through me. I freeze, my breath catching in my throat, my brain momentarily forgetting how to inhale. Everything around me stops; the background noise of the pub fades into oblivion until all I can hear is the relentless thump of my heart. The world narrows down to this single moment, to the feel of his lips against my ear, to the warmth of his breath. Then, his voice blankets even the sound of my heartbeat, enveloping me completely, and I am lost in the sensation.

"Macey took care of my table, Angel, so I guess I'll be seeing you on Christmas Day." Fuck me. His head pulls back slightly, so he is staring at me, his gaze piercing my very soul. His fingers tighten on my hips as his nostrils flare and his eyes flicker to my lips as he squeezes my hips again, causing a gasp to leave me. He eases up and delicately traces over the spot he was just touching. His head moves again, his breath fanning my neck.

"To express my appreciation for getting us in, I'll bring you candy canes." His husky voice sends what I can only describe as fireworks going off inside me right now. Every single hair on my body goes to a standing point and I squeeze my legs together as tight as possible, already feeling the wetness between them. The feel of his fingers disappears as I watch him vanish into the crowd. I'm left speechless and feeling as if I'm being consumed by fire. My body's response to his touch is undeniable, as evidenced by the lingering tingle on my hips and the intense sensations between my legs.

Chapter Eight

Carter

Christmas Day

It's been ten days since I last laid eyes on her. Our last encounter, when I touched her, felt like an eruption of heated lust within me. My fingers tingled for days afterward. Even now, I can still feel the ghost of her skin beneath my fingertips, a haunting reminder of our brief contact. I've wrapped those exact fingers around my dick at the thought of her, wishing it was her skin wrapped around it and not my hand.

I'm in a taxi heading to the pub, my mind completely consumed by the thought of seeing her again. Every second that passes heightens my anticipation. Seeing Angel at Costco was the confirmation I needed. She's a woman now, and I need her. It's as simple as that. I can sense her attraction for me in the way her eyes trace my every move, the way her breath hitches when I'm near. Her ability to form a coherent sentence vanishes when she's in my presence, and I can see the struggle in her eyes as she tries to maintain her composure.

The memory of her touch is seared into my mind, and the thought of feeling her skin again sends a shiver down my spine. I know she feels the same pull, the same magnetic attraction that I do. The way she looked at me, the way her body responded to my touch, it was undeniable. I need to see her, to feel her, to confirm that this connection between us is real and not just a figment of my imagination.

I intend to create a Christmas she'll never forget, and I will outdo every guy she's ever been with. I hunger for Angel to crave me with the same intensity that I crave her. I want her to wake up every day with thoughts of me, just like I do with her. Each night, she'll find solace pleasuring herself while focusing solely on the way I satisfy her—no one else.

"What's inside that bag, son?" my dad questions.

I suppress my smile, maintaining a neutral expression while contemplating the large candy cane I purchased for Angel. Although it will take days to finish, I couldn't resist buying it when I saw it.

"I know the owner of the pub. I just got them a little thank you for getting us in at such short notice," I say, hoping he won't ask what's inside because a jumbo candy cane doesn't scream 'thank you', but I know it will make Angel smile.

He smacks my knee. "Carter, you're a fine lad," he whispers, while gazing out the window as we cross London Bridge.

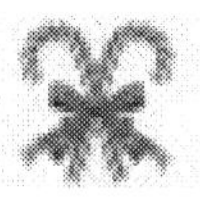

The pub is crowded with customers and I have yet to spot Angel in the twenty minutes since we were seated. *Is she deliberately trying to avoid me?* The thought alone has me grinding my teeth together with the need to go find her. Before I can do such a thing, the waiter arrives with the drinks we ordered. As he places my glass on the table, I discreetly grab his attention. "Is Angel around today?" I inquire, attempting to hide my enthusiasm. His reaction is a frown of confusion, as if caught off guard.

"Uh, yeah. She's starting soon with Mace. They are just out back. Are you her uncle or something?" Assessing me with narrowed eyes, he stares at me as if he's trying to figure out if he recognises me. I'm annoyed by his assumption. Cheeky fucker.

"I'm definitely not her uncle," I seethe angrily.

He widens his eyes, bringing his hands up in surrender. "Sorry, man. I didn't mean to offend. Do you want me to go get her?" he rushes out, placing Ty's drink down. Casting a quick glance at Tyson, who observes this scenario play out with interest. My brother holds on tightly to things, similar to a dog with a bone. I shouldn't have thought it was wise to investigate anything with him there.

I shake my head. "No need, you're good. Don't worry," I mumble, and the boy nods, making his way further round the table with everyone's drinks.

"What was that about?" Ty's question comes quicker than expected.

I take a sip of my beer and reply with a simple, "nothing."

Ty chuckles. "Bro, you're not getting away that easily. Nice try though."

I cast a doubtful look at him and let out a sigh, fully aware that he won't drop it until I tell him what he wants to know. "I know someone that works here, that's all." With a casual shrug, I drink more of my beer. If he continues to interrogate me, I'll chug the pint in two seconds flat.

"Who?" He contorts his face in confusion, as if he should know all of my friends.

"You don't know them." I won't mention her, in the hope that it will make him drop the subject. His slow nodding and constant scanning of the room suggests he will be scrutinising every server that approaches to figure out who it is.

The challenge of growing up with four brothers is finding new ways to get under each other's skin. Additionally, our knowledge of one another is as familiar as our own hands. Strangely, Tyson understands me better than anyone else.

Being the second oldest, I played a big role in helping Mum and Dad raise Tyson, who is twelve years younger than me. Amongst my brothers, Ty and I have the strongest bond, and he knows me well enough to understand that there's only one reason I'm here today: because of a girl. I regret not choosing a seat at the opposite end of the table. It's not about him not caring or judging me, it's about him constantly bringing it up and causing others to become suspicious, which I don't want, especially on Christmas Day.

As he finishes handing out the drinks, the server enquires, "Are you all set for your starters?"

After receiving nods from everyone around the table, he walks off towards the kitchen. I observe the doors opening and closing, and just as I go to turn around, they swing open once more, and there she stands.

Fuck me. She is the epitome of what every guy dreams about.

I can only see her upper half due to one side of the bar blocking her bottom half, but her sexy elf attire leaves me feeling breathless. *How can I get through lunch with her looking like that?* Her hair cascades down her front and she's rocking a green hat with a red trim. I see a tube-style dress or top without arms that accentuates her perky breasts.

She can't be walking around like this today. I watch her closely, and when that lanky jerk shows up again, he emits a wolf whistle that makes me want to punch something. While I've never contemplated hurting anyone, I can't deny that I'm not against the idea when it comes to him. The way he looks at her makes his attraction towards her plain for everyone to see. *Are they together? Have they been together in the past?* The thought fills me with an unmatched fury. Wait. I knew I recognised him. He's that fucking shit that had his arm over her shoulder in the picture on her social media. Fury isn't even what I would describe me as now. I could spit fucking fire right now. I clutch the arm of the chair I'm sitting in just to keep me seated so I don't storm over there and do something I regret.

Angel rolls her eyes, walking to the side of the bar, and leans over to grab something from behind it. She straightens back up and walks around to the front. I see all of her and everything around me fades away.

Ty's voice comes from behind me. "Oh, brother. You're fucked."

Chapter Nine

Angel

As I assess my reflection in the mirror, I can't help but cringe at the hideous costume Mace chose—it's so not suitable for a family Christmas Day lunch.

Nevertheless, she tossed a pair of ugly green tights at me and claimed they would make the outfit more family-friendly. I feel more like a tree than an elf, but I'll do anything to silence Mace's complaints, even if it's just for a day.

I woke up to the sound of Mace screeching out songs outside my bedroom door at 6 am. I anticipated that she would wake me up with terrible Christmas songs, so I blocked my bedroom door with my desk before she could think about coming into my room and giving me an unwanted front-row seat to her performance. Once I heard her high-pitched wailing, I promptly inserted my noise-cancelling headphones, set my phone to airplane mode so she couldn't blow it up with calls and texts, and peacefully dozed off until my alarm blared through my headphones at 8 am, signalling the arrival of the most dreadful day of the year.

Mace was furious that I'd slept so late and was downstairs already, dancing wildly in the empty pub to Michael Bublé at full volume. For a whole fifteen minutes, she completely ignored my existence before throwing my outfit at me.

Me and Mace have been rushing around all morning making sure everything was ready and prepared for our customers. Even though I've been completely rushed off my feet, I've been trying everything I can do to mentally block out Mr Hayes; pretending he's not here, but I can sense him without even looking. Once I come face-to-face with him, it's game over. I'll be a spluttering mess and will barely be able to carry a plate. He sends my mind and body into disarray with just one look. Fortunately, we have assigned serving staff to their own quarter of the restaurant and since I knew Mr Hayes' whereabouts, I deliberately chose the furthest spot in the restaurant.

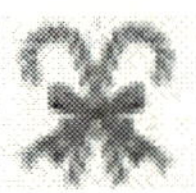

The day is going well despite the festive atmosphere, constant holiday greetings, and the repeated question of what I got for Christmas. If this wasn't my family's pub, I'd probably reveal exactly what Mace brought me: a clit suction stimulator that will make me see stars in every galaxy. I don't tell them that though, instead I keep it professional and smile while trying to awkwardly change the conversation.

"Ang, would you mind watching the bar for a bit, please? It's getting pretty hectic," Mace shouts in my direction. "I'll take care of your side," she adds. Although the dinner is sit-down, we're maintaining the pub vibe by allowing people to mingle at the bar after they've eaten. Without even answering her, I take the empty plates I was collecting from a table, place them in the open hatch to the kitchen, and then make my way over to the bar. Mace is right; it's heaving, and poor Michael is on his own. I step behind the bar and begin serving customers by taking their orders. After a while, things start to calm down and the bar becomes quieter.

As Michael walks towards me, he throws his arm casually over my shoulder. "Carry me. I'm dying on my feet," he jokes as he lets half his weight hang on me. As I stumble to the side, my knees give way, and I tumble to the floor. Michael and I burst into laughter as he helps me up and pulls me close again.

As "All I Want for Christmas" plays, we dance behind the bar, my arms encircling his waist. Even though I don't enjoy Christmas, I have to maintain a smile throughout a long day and an even longer night. It's easy with Michael. When he joined the company four years ago, we instantly had a strong bond.

Someone clears their throat, and then there's a voice that, with all the chaos of today, I forgot about, interrupts my thoughts.

"Can I get some service?"

I pivot on my heels and come face to face with the one person I desperately wanted to avoid today. My stomach churns, my body flooding with a rush of warmth. My insides flutter with butterflies as I take a moment to take him in. He looks absolutely stunning in a stylish black buttoned-up shirt, with his dark brown hair expertly styled and swept back, except for a loose strand that falls over his eyes. I feel paralyzed from his gaze as he holds me in place.

"Can I help?" Michael asks, oblivious to the moment Mr Hayes and I are having.

"A JD and coke." Even as he speaks, Mr Hayes' gaze remains fixed on me. Michael hesitates before turning around and rolls his eyes at me, likely due to Mr Hayes' rude tone.

"That order wasn't intended for you," Mr Hayes barks, still not taking his eyes off me. Although my eyes widen, I resist the urge to retaliate against the snap in his voice. In a trance-like state, I turn my back on him, finally breaking our connection, and pry the glass from Michael's tightly clenched hand.

"I don't appreciate you speaking to my colleague like that," Michael grits out.

"Michael, it's fine. I know him." I offer my friend a smile, my lips sealed tightly as I walk past the rows of spirits clinging to the wall.

"Double, Angel," Mr Hayes adds with a dull tone.

Michael crowds me from behind. "You don't need to take this shit from this joker. If you want, I can remove the old man," he says a bit too loudly.

I shake my head in reply. "Honestly, it's fine. I'm used to this sort of thing." I try to laugh it off. "I got this. Do you want to go and help Mace on the floor?" I place my hand on Michael's arm and offer him a small smile, trying to communicate that everything is okay. With a slow nod, he glances at Mr Hayes and then back at me before making his way out from behind the bar.

With the spirit poured, I turn back to face the man I'm trying to avoid. "Tell me when to stop." Placing the Coke tap in the glass, I begin to fill.

A second later, Mr Hayes commands me to stop, with just a tiny amount of Coke in the glass. He might as well have been without any. I set the glass down in front of him and give him a stern look, questioning his sudden rudeness towards me.

"£9, please." I put my hand out, and Mr Hayes pulls out a £20. He holds it a little away from my hand.

"Join me." He tilts his head to the side, his gaze running down the length of me slowly, his stare setting my whole body alight.

"I like your cute outfit, Angel." His eyes land back on mine, but this time, his golden irises have darkened to a captivating brown. "Much more revealing than your old school uniform." I gasp at the thought of him remembering me in my school attire. I have no experience with guys, but I'm pretty sure that his current look definitely shows desire.

"I don't drink while working." I lean forward, snatching the £20 out of his hand, and walk towards the till.

I attempt to calm my racing heart by taking subtle, deep breaths. *Why does this happen whenever he's around me?*

I set the change on the bar in front of him and call out to Mace. "Just stepping away for a quick break." She gives me a thumbs-up and goes back to what she was doing. Without sparing Mr Hayes a second look, I walk out the back and let the doors slam behind me. Once I'm no longer visible, I clutch the edges of the table in the back room and breathe deeply. He has the power to make me melt with a single glance, leaving me desperate for his touch. I'm in dire need of that suction toy at the moment.

"Fuck," I mutter, looking up at the ceiling, hoping for some sort of miracle.

"I really want you to have that drink with me, Angel." I look to the mirror in front of me to find Mr Hayes's reflection, looking at me as if I were his next meal.

I exhale and utter, "Mr Hayes?...What..." I can't even form a sentence to ask him why he's back here.

He approaches me slowly, like a wild beast stalking his prey. I should be telling him he's not meant to be back here; I should be asking him nicely to get back to the bar; I should be worried that, at any minute, Mace could walk back here and demand to know what's going on, but I can't. I'm powerless to break free from the mesmerising effect he has whenever his eyes are on me.

Standing behind me, Mr Hayes is so close that I can feel my arse brushing against his thighs as he looms over me.

"Tilt your head backwards," he commands, never averting his eyes from mine. I frown, but with a single raised eyebrow, he communicates a clear message: don't question me. Maybe it's because he was my teacher for years, but I trust him, so I tilt my head back until I'm staring at the ceiling.

His lips ghost the shell of my ear. "Open your mouth." I do as I'm told, but my pounding heart betrays me as my breathing becomes a lot more rapid. There is no doubt that he knows the effect he has on me. I remain silent, mouth open, chest heaving, waiting for this next move.

"I just wanted you to have a drink with me, Angel," he softly murmurs in my ear. He moves and suddenly the glass of JD and minimal coke I prepared for him hovers above my face. He tilts it and the ice-cold liquid hits my tongue.

"Swallow." Drinking without choking is a challenge because of the angle of my head, but I manage it. However, some of the liquid escapes my mouth and runs down my neck. The glass disappears, and then I feel him. He trails his lips and tongue along my neck. I can't help my gasp as the sensation sends a signal straight to my core. Thoughts of his mouth in other places consume me, intensifying the ache between my thighs. He brings his lips back to my ear.

"You make it taste so much better."

Chapter Ten

Carter

Throughout the day, I observed her flirting with that jerk who questioned if I was her uncle. I came to this place because of her. Seeing her was all I wanted. If I couldn't read her like a book, I might have thought she wasn't interested, but that wasn't the case. My presence makes her feel intimidated. I realised I had to be the one to make the first move, but as I approached the bar, I saw that skinny guy with her in his arms. Rage and jealousy swarmed me. It made me want to bend her over the bar and show everyone who she belongs to.

I wanted to ask her about her Christmas and what she had planned after the pub closed tonight, but seeing her with *him* made me reconsider. She could dance around with him, but she couldn't even socialise over a drink with her ex-English teacher. So here I am, making her. The taste of the JD I licked from her neck lingers on my tongue. My dick throbs from finally getting this close to her, tasting her, although it's not really how I want to be tasting her.

“Mr Hayes,” she moans. The way she addresses me as Mr Hayes makes me intensely fucking hard. I had dreams of her moaning ‘Mr Hayes’, but my dreams were no match to the way it sounds. I now crave hearing it over and over.

“Angel, I need you,” I whisper into her ear. I’m not holding it back anymore; she has to know how much I crave her. Spinning her around, I place the now empty glass on the table. “I need you now.” I don’t even give her a second to react. I grasp her cheeks and press my lips to hers. She responds by raking her fingers through my hair, tugging so hard that my eyes water. Our tongues intertwine as she moans and presses herself against me, causing me to grip her arse cheeks and squeeze them.

“Angel,” I growl against her lips as she continues to rub against me, making me feel like I'm about to explode.

She pulls away, looking up at me with hooded eyes that are irresistibly sexy. “Mr Hayes,” she moans.

“Where’s your room?” I refuse to wait any longer. I need Angel O’Sullivan, and I need her now. There's a moment of realisation in her expression as my words sink in.

“I—uh.” Her face and her cheeks flame red, followed by a clear look of fear dancing in her eyes.

“Angel, if you don’t want this, you just have to say,” I assure her.

“No, no. I do. I have wanted this for so long. I swear, Mr Hayes. I just need to get back to work. It’s too busy out there for me to just vanish and leave them short-staffed." Suddenly, her face falls as if it dawned on her what she's just said.

"Is this something you've been wanting for a long time?" I playfully tease while playing with the loose strand of hair hanging loose from her ponytail. I didn't think her cheeks could become more flushed, yet they do. She lowers her head, but I gently lift her chin with my finger, noticing her eyes are shut.

"Open your eyes, Angel." I lower my voice and gently press my lips to her left cheek. "I thought about you more than I'd care to admit" Her body tenses and she inhales sharply. I move and press my lips against her right cheek. "I've imagined you on your knees for me." She gasps, her breaths becoming faster and more uneven. I gently kiss her on the forehead. "I daydreamed about your plump lips on my cock, as you satisfy me."

A moan escapes her lips and I need to taste her again, so I press my mouth to hers, running my tongue along her lips coaxing her to open for me and when she does, my tongue moves against hers, intertwining as they dance around each other. I can't get enough of her and now I have her like this, there's no way I can let her go. Images of her flash through my mind that I conjured through my fantasies. I need her. Breaking our connection, I pull back slightly as her desire stares back at me with her blown wide eyes. "And I thought about you screaming 'Mr Hayes' when I bury myself deep in that tight, wet pussy. Now text Mace and tell her you're not feeling well and have gone to lie down," I grit out.

Angel nods eagerly and quickly retrieves her phone from her bra. "It was quietening down out there; they will be fine," I reassure her. As she types, I observe her biting her lip and hesitating. "Where's your room?" I ask again. When she gestures towards the door, I seize her hand and walk towards it. Without hesitation, she lets me take control and guide us. Angel moves in front of me, ascending the stairs. I observe the way her hips sway and notice the little elf dress riding up and becoming shorter. She opens the door to her flat and we go inside.

"No lock?" I question as I close the door behind me. Her response is a nod.

"We don't bother locking it when we're downstairs," she explains, heading towards what must be her room. Walking by another door, I swiftly glance inside. Covered in baubles and lights, a colossal pink tree fills their living room. I smirk because Angel must detest it.

"Someone could sneak up here unnoticed. You should keep it locked," I suggest. Turning towards me, her eyes widen as if she's been reprimanded by her father, and then she acknowledges with a nod.

"Okay." Her submission fills me with joy and makes my heart swell. I'm a fan of it. I wonder what else I could ask her to do.

As we step into her room, a small smile appears on my face. It's a simple room, furnished with a king-size bed, desk and wardrobe. Standing by the edge of her bed, she absentmindedly picks at her nails while staring down at the floor. I walk towards her and place my finger under her chin, directing her attention towards me. The moment her green eyes twinkle up at me, the world disappears. I pause to take a deep breath, bothered by the discomfort in my chest. This moment is what I have been waiting for, for so long and I almost thought I would never be here and have this moment with her. It doesn't feel real.

I gently bring my lips to Angel's and kiss her. I use my tongue to press against her lips, seeking entrance. I don't rush it; I kiss her slowly, conveying that I'll go at the pace she wants. I can't get enough of her. I'm undoubtedly desperate for Angel. Her taste, her smell, her moans. I want it all.

I want Angel to feel as desperate for me as I do for her.

I want her to go crazy with need with every swipe of my tongue the way I do hers.

I don't think there is a drug out there more intoxicating than Angel O'Sullivan.

She's an addiction I never want to lose and a fix I'll crave for the rest of my life. I gently move away. A frown mars her face, as if me pulling away makes her unhappy, which only serves to make me smile. Her big, hooded eyes meet mine. “Since when have you wanted this?” I question. Contrary to my expectations, she doesn't hide away.

“Way longer than I should have,” she admits. “I think about you a lot,” she continues. Hearing this sends a surge of pride to my chest.

“How have you thought about me?” I want to know how she thinks about me and when. What does she do? I am eager to learn every detail. Her head tilts down as if she can’t hold eye contact with me, her shyness still clear. “Angel,” I mumble. “Tell me. I told you the things I’ve been thinking about you.” I remind her of what I said downstairs.

“I've had lots of fantasies about you,” she confesses. Her chest moves up and down at a rapid pace as if she's in a heightened state, thinking back to those fantasies as we speak. Her hooded eyes are mirroring exactly how I'm feeling.

“You've had fantasies about me?” I question her. It feels like all the blood is heading south and pooling in my cock, hardening with every second and becoming uncomfortable against my jeans’ zipper. Her mouth opens slightly as if it’s come too much for her to breathe through her nose. She nods, not breaking eye contact, but my favourite cherry-red stain graces her cheeks.

"Show me," I demand, not taking my eyes off her. Her confidence doesn't waver, but her face creases with a frown.

Her eyebrows furrow and her face scrunches slightly as she asks, "What?" Her eyes anxiously dance between mine, as if she's anticipating my explanation. Her innocence tempts me to loosen my restraint and bury myself deep inside her while I bend her in fucking half until she screams my name, but I have to go slow. If I lose control, I'll completely ruin her.

"Show me how you fantasise about me." I force myself to speak, attempting to regain control. With bulging eyes, she opens and closes her mouth multiple times.

"Uh..."

She looks like a deer caught in headlights. Her body trembles visibly as I lightly brush my lips against her ear. "I want to see every movement and hear every moan that leaves those sweet lips when you think of me, Angel."

Chapter Eleven

Angel

He wants me to show him.

I can't.

I can barely put together a sentence in front of this guy. How can I show him what I do when thinking about him? His dark eyes lock onto mine, no longer filled with their golden hue. I move my head in a side-to-side motion. I feel so humiliated that I want to cry, but I can't physically do it. My body won't let me do anything.

"I can't." I bow my head, silently pleading that my tears stay hidden. He is aware of my age, but why must I be so inexperienced? My deepest fantasies could become a reality now, but I can't even pleasure myself for him.

"Angel, eyes on me." His soft voice begins to soothe my inner turmoil. I tilt my head up, avoiding direct eye contact by looking slightly past him. His eyes have a profound effect on me, making me feel incredibly vulnerable.

"Angel, it's okay. Why don't you share with me what you do, and I'll take care of it." His voice cracks as he utters the final words. I watch how his chest rapidly expands and his hands tightly clench into fists. Once again, this man leaves me speechless and I can only nod my head. With a gentle hand on my shoulder he pushes me into a seated position on the bed.

"Angel, what do you want me to do first?" His rough voice sends shivers down my spine as I glance up at him.

"Ki-kiss me," I stutter. I remain unconvinced of the reality of this. Mr Hayes bends over me, guiding me to lay down. Our lips meet instantly in a slow, passionate kiss, our tongues entwining in a captivating dance.

"What now?" He breathes harshly. The physical sensation of his loss of control, as his body trembles over me, boosts my confidence.

"Kiss down my body."

A slight groan escapes his lips as he kisses his way down my body, starting from my lips and moving to my jawline and neck. Gradually, he moves down my neck, pausing when he reaches my dress, his gaze travelling down my body.

"I need you, naked. Now," he desperately begs as he yanks my arm out of the dress at an awkward angle, like he can't wait a moment longer. The realisation of what is happening hits me. *Shit.*

"Carter, I—"

He momentarily freezes before his hands cradle my face. "What's my name, Angel?" I only called him Carter to appear more mature, but the truth is, I love calling him Mr Hayes, and he clearly enjoys it as well.

"M—Mr Hayes."

"Mmm." He caresses my cheeks with his thumbs. "Don't call me Carter, Angel."

"Yes, Mr Hayes." He inhales deeply, closing his eyes and tilting his head back.

"Such a good girl for me, Angel." His hand glides down the front of my dress, then in one swift motion, he pulls, and I hear a tear as the dress slips away. The torn fabric lays under me, never to be worn again.

My tights are caught by his hooked fingers and then they're shredded material laying on the floor. My body heats as I watch his gaze cruise over me, taking in my white lacy bra and thong. I'm not as uncomfortable as I expected being exposed like this. I feel like the perfect picture for him.

"Angel, you have no idea how patiently I've been waiting for this." His lips graze my collarbone as he showers it with delicate kisses. He glides his fingers along the edge of my bra and swiftly pulls it down in one fluid motion. My boobs bounce free, and he cups them with his large hands, his fingers twisting and flicking my hard nipples, causing my breath to hitch. Squirming on the bed, my back arches.

In a hushed and gravelly voice, he asks, "Angel, do you like when my fingers brush over these perfect nipples?"

"Yes," I tell him honestly.

“What about if I suck?” He doesn’t wait for my response, as a warm, wet feeling envelopes my nipple as his tongue swirls around it. His teeth graze and bite down slightly; the pain from the sharp sting is dulled by the ache in my core.

“Mr Hayes,” I moan.

“I know, Angel. I know.” His warm breath on my nipples causes me to grasp his hair tightly. It’s all too much; the sensations are taking over my body, and I can’t tell where they start or end. I’ve never felt like this before.

Mr Hayes moves away from my breasts and begins a slow journey down to my belly. He reaches my waist and plants a soft kiss on either side of my hipbones before sliding his fingers into my thong and removing it. My heart beats so loudly that everything else becomes barely audible. I can feel my own wetness between my thighs, but Mr Hayes prevents me from closing my legs by positioning his knee in the space between them. I’m too embarrassed to even look at him, keeping my eyes firmly closed. I know this is normal for me; I’m always wet. It's constant, even when I'm not aroused, but when I do get aroused, it feels like a tap has been turned on.

“Don’t shy away from me, Angel. I want to see this pretty pussy.” Mr Hayes’s fingers creep up my leg, the pulse in my clit is stronger than it ever has been before, and I swear the ache in my core, travels all the way through to my arse. Once his fingers touch the outer lips, he lets out a loud moan.

"Fuck, you're soaked." He teasingly runs two fingers between my folds. "Please tell me I taste this sweet cunt in your fantasies, Angel, because if I don't, just know I'm creating a new one for you right now." Mr Hayes drops to his knees and wraps his forearms around my waist, pulling me so my arse hangs off the bed. My calves are positioned on his shoulders, his hands firmly grasping my arse. Suspended mid-air, my mind can't catch up before his fast tongue starts flicking over my swollen clit, sending me into a blissful heaven. I can't even comprehend the words coming out of my mouth. I've never experienced a sensation like this before. It gradually intensifies until his tongue enters and exits my opening. There's an unsettling sensation that I just can't shake from the depths of my mind.

He doesn't know I'm a virgin.

Mr Hayes halts, his tongue no longer inside me and the peak he was taking me to disappears. I want to scream and beg for him to touch me, lick me again, but he conceals his hands behind me as he lets my body descend onto the bed. As my legs slip off his shoulders, the heels of my feet make contact with the bed. I lay there, legs tightly held together, knees pointing up, mesmerised as he removes his shirt. I feel as if the floor will vanish beneath me.

His body is absolute perfection. He has a toned physique, but not to the extreme where he appears obsessed with the gym; just enough to show he takes care of himself. The sight of his broad shoulders and toned arms confirms his commitment to exercise, yet my focus is immediately drawn to the sculpted V in his hips, causing a sudden tightening sensation in my legs. Surprisingly, it ignited a newfound wave of desire in me. I'm surprised by how much hair he has. From his chest, it travels downward along his torso, creating a thick line that disappears beneath his trousers. He is all man, and this is what I want. I don't want a boy; I want a man. I suddenly feel a dryness in my mouth as I swallow. I need to say something.

"Mr Hayes," I say, as a smile graces his glistening lips from all my juices, and he leans to the side of the bed and picks something up.

"I completely forgot, but I have something for you." He produces a small red paper bag. I didn't even notice he was carrying that. Something is poking out of it, but I'm unsure of what it is. He pulls it out and my face turns into a frown, but then it dawns on me. There's a jumbo candy cane with a red bow wrapped around it.

"I spotted this and thought you'd appreciate it, but now I'm craving it too." A sly smile emerges as he begins to unwrap it. I look puzzled, trying to understand why he suddenly craves candy cane. My eyes dart back and forth between him and the sugary treat as I try to figure out what's going on. After removing the wrapping, he places it next to me on the bed, and then his fingers playfully travel up my legs and come to rest on my knees. With a slow motion, he moves them away from each other.

"When you think of me, do you rub this sweet nub?" Mr Hayes applies pressure to my clit with his thumb, causing me to moan and throw my head back.

"Or does your finger effortlessly slide into this tight opening?" he asks, as one finger glides into my wet pussy. My body immediately tenses. While I do finger myself, his hands are significantly larger than mine. What if he somehow takes my virginity while fingering me? Can that even happen?

"Answer me, Angel." I am snapped out of my internal thoughts by his stern voice.

I exhale and manage to say, "Ye-Yes." One finger enters, followed by the sensation of stretching when he includes a second one.

"Fuck, Angel. You're tight." He removes both and then inserts them again. *Shit. Shit.* His fingers vanish, and moments later, I experience a sensation at my entrance, followed by an overwhelming stretch. *Oh, my God. He's entering me, and I haven't told him. I'm a virgin. Oh, my God.*

"Mr Hayes." He doesn't push himself all the way in; instead, he pulls out.

"Have you ever tasted yourself with candy, Angel?" *With candy? What is he going on—*

He holds the jumbo candy cane to his mouth and licks it. Frowning, I watch as he lowers it again, and then I'm aware of him sliding it into me. My desire intensifies again as he pulls it back out and licks it once more. This has got to be the hottest thing I have ever seen.

“Are you going to show me how well you can take this before you take me?” Mr Hayes pushes it into me a lot deeper this time. I instantly tighten, which makes the candy cane slip in deeper. My arousal is clear by the noise with each gentle thrust.

“Stop, Mr Hayes.” As I exhale, I clutch the bedsheets next to me. I relax by closing my eyes and taking long, calming breaths.

“Angel?” Mr Hayes's voice breaks through with worry, and I sense the candy cane vanishing.

“There's something you should know,” I say with my eyes shut. In a hushed tone, I confess, “I'm a virgin.” There is complete silence. The thought of Mr Hayes looking at me in disgust makes it hard for me to open my eyes. *Does he think I intentionally lured him here so I could lose my virginity? Does he believe this is merely a game? Will he view me through the lens of my past as a young high school girl? Is he going to put his shirt back on, stand up, and leave?*

I inhale deeply, then open my eyes. Mr Hayes catches me off guard with his intense stare. The expression isn't the disgusted one I had in mind. With his piercing gaze, he searches my face, kindling a passionate fire in the depths of my stomach until his smile extinguishes the flame.

Chapter Twelve

Carter

She's a virgin.

Her body has remained untouched by anyone.

Her untamed eyes flicker between mine, like she's anxiously awaiting my response. Her actions are a perfect reflection of her name.

She's an absolute angel.

"How?" I furrow my brows. "Angel, how is it possible that you're still a virgin? You're perfect in every way. Boys must fall at your feet." She lowers her head and lets out a sigh of relief.

"Yes, some boys." Her piercing green eyes lock onto mine, delving deep into my soul. "But they're boys. They were never you, Mr Hayes."

Her voice is causing my erection to get harder. If that's even possible. I am certain that she was sent to this world with the sole intention of ending my life. She has never appeared so flawlessly perfect. I know I shouldn't, but I can't leave without leaving my mark on Angel. No man is now claiming what's mine.

"Well, then, Angel." My unfiltered voice emerges from my overwhelmed mind. "Let me show you how a man can make you feel." Pools of desire stare back at me as she slowly nods. Her lips curl up in a small smile. She tilts her head back onto the bed, her hair forming gentle waves. I'm glad she told me she was a virgin. *If I had pushed that candy cane in any further, could it have taken her virtue? Could I have pulled it out, and blood would have stained it?* As I grip her thighs tightly, she lets out a stuttered gasp. I only want to see that blood staining my dick, nothing else.

Her blood is mine.

"You know this might hurt, Angel." I fix her with an intense gaze. Her face still displays a dreamy smile while she looks at me as if I am her god, and in this moment, I truly feel like one. "But you trust me, don't you? You trust me to make you feel good, even if it might be too much at first?" A frown mars her face as she frantically nods.

"I trust you, Mr Hayes." I tilt my head upwards, blinking at the ceiling momentarily, attempting to clear my mind of thoughts about her. I can't let her think I'm like the eighteen-year-olds she's avoiding, even though her words and innocence are enticing. With a long, forceful breath, I return my gaze to Angel.

I lower myself, planting a line of kisses along her jawline before landing on her lips.

"Angel, where have you been?" I whisper, savouring this moment, hoping it stays with me forever.

"Waiting for you, Mr Hayes." Her silken voice has every hair on my body standing to a sharp point. I let out a groan and stand up beside the bed, quickly undoing the buttons on my jeans. Lowering them, I notice Angel watching me intently, resting on her elbows. Despite the fact that I still have my boxers on, I am fully erect and it is poking out of the top of my waistband. Her eyes don't move from my dick; her chest heaves as she takes deep breaths, probably wondering how I'm going to fit inside her. I'm slightly above average in size, but I'm also thick. I realise I need to handle her delicately since she was tight with just my two fingers.

"Trust me?" Without any hesitation, she vigorously nods her head.

"Angel, did these thoughts exist in your imagination? Did you allow yourself to be mine in your fantasies?" I have to know if she thought of me fucking her.

"Every single time, Mr Hayes." I don't think I'm ever letting her go. How can I? I slide my boxers down and watch as her chest heaves with exaggerated breaths. I place myself between her legs, my eyes fixated on her glistening cunt.

"Has anyone touched you, Angel?" She shakes her head. Her purity is unmatched, and I consider myself the luckiest man alive to be the man who she gives this to. The fact that I'm the first makes me feral.

"Are you on anything?" I question.

"The pill," she rushes out, and I frown in question but she quickly follows up, "I-uh, get bad periods." Her cheeks flame red and I've come to accept that Angel red is my new favourite colour, and I want to see her flush every moment she is around me.

"Angel, I've always used protection, but I want to feel you. I want to feel every pulse of your cunt as it comes around my dick. I want your juices dripping off me." I fixate my gaze on her, watching her reaction.

"Yes," she stutters.

I narrow my eyes. "Yes, what?" It's as though she's having an internal debate, her mouth opening and closing in response.

"Yes, Daddy." As she studies my expression, my eyes widen, and the reaction becomes evident in the throbbing pulse and leaking pre-cum from my dick. The moment she utters those words, I grab her arms, pinning her down and kissing her passionately. I consume every noise she lets slip from her mouth. I want her to call me Daddy every day of her fucking life. *Fuck.*

"Angel," I growl. "What are you doing to me?" I need to be inside her. I can't wait any longer. I tightly grip my dick and glide it along her wetness, collecting her arousal. Her responsiveness is captivating as she mewls and flings her head back.

"Angel, I want your eyes on me when I enter you. I want you to watch me when I take what's mine."

With gritted teeth and a deep breath, I push the tip of my cock inside her warm, wet walls. *Fucking hell, she is tight.* Despite squinting her eyes, she obediently keeps her gaze fixed on me. I push myself in deeper. Her cunt feels like a vice lock around my dick, and all I want to do is pound into her and hear her screams, but I have to be slow. Now that I'm halfway in, I can see her eyes welling up with tears.

"Trust me, Angel?" She confirms she understands with a nod, but doesn't say anything. I continue to push deeper.

"Mr Hayes." A pained cry leaves her. I can't wait this out any longer. I push myself in fully and she cries out. "It's too much. It hurts."

"You can take it, Angel. You can take it for your daddy, can't you?" With reassuring words, I calm her down, her cries soon transforming into moans. As I watch my dick move in and out of her tight cunt, I apply a gentle amount of pressure to her clit with my thumb.

"Look how well you're taking me, Angel. Your cunt was made for me, wasn't it?" She lets out a loud gasp while wrapping her legs around my back. I increase the depth and speed up my movements as her body relaxes, and she seems to take me with more ease. Sweat droplets shimmer on her forehead while she clings to the sheets. I increase the speed and move my thumb in circular motions on her clit.

"Mr Hayes, oh my God." She arches her back off the bed, her legs gripping me tightly, and a scream of pleasure escapes her lips. I witness her trembling form as she cums, causing her skin to break out in goosebumps. Her sweet cunt flutters around my dick. She's an unforgettable vision that I never want to lose.

"That's it, come for your daddy, Angel." I drop my thumb from her clit and slow down my thrusts into her. I don't want this to end and I will drag it out as long as possible. She relaxes and lets herself fall back onto the bed, her breathing slowing and her legs releasing their grip on me.

"My fantasies could never match that," she exhales. Her face breaks into a lazy smile. I withdraw from her, and she lets out a hiss. Although I know she's sore, I cannot end here.

I need more of her.

"Angel, I'm not done with you yet. Can you take more?"

While I don't want her to suffer, I believe the pleasure will suppress any pain.

"Yes, Mr Hayes." As I peer down at my dick, smeared with blood and see it on her legs, an urge to behave like a savage surges through me, accompanied by a sudden feeling. I want to taste her in every way possible.

"I crave your taste, Angel," I murmur, sinking to the floor and eagerly indulge in her cunt. I slide my tongue into her opening, licking the inner walls as she moans softly once more. I use the sticky candy cane to flick against her clit while pleasuring her with my tongue repeatedly. I shut my eyes and relish her completely, as if she's my last meal. Her taste is hands down the most delicious thing I've ever experienced.

"Your innocence tastes so sweet, Angel." I spit on her clit and lick it back up. I notice blood on the candy cane, causing me to reach out to her.

"Taste how sweet you are, Angel." It's not like me, but she has a way of making me feral and bringing out a sweet yet twisted side in me. Without any hesitation, she simply accepts it, wrapping her lips around it, sucking, licking.

"Fuck, Angel." I toss the candy cane and sit up. This time, I place her legs over my shoulders and lean over her so her hard nipples brush my chest. I fantasised about having her bent in half with my dick buried in her tight, wet pussy, and now I'm going to have it.

My dick is throbbing, and her pussy dripping. I allow my dick to slide through her folds, making sure I brush the head over her swollen clit. She stutters on a breath before I position myself at her entrance.

Our panting breaths mingle together as our noses brush one another. Her hooded eyes go wide as I slowly push myself in. I have to close my eyes and take a deep breath; her walls tighten around me instantly like a fucking glove I never want to take off. I can't come already, but her pussy is trying everything it can to milk my cock for every last drop.

I open my eyes and my heart skips a beat. Her emerald eyes roll back with every gentle thrust, her lips open slightly with small mews leaving her mouth. Every time my chest brushes against her nipples, I feel her pussy flutter. My stomach flips with every second that goes by. She's fucking mine. I'm never letting her leave. Wherever she will go, I will be there, whether or not she accepts it.

The thought causes me to drive into her relentlessly, filling her to the hilt, I bring my hands up to her face and cradle her cheeks, holding her in place, hoping she can bear the pain from the sharp thrusts, but by the looks of her, the pleasure is numbing the pain completely.

I drop my forehead to hers and close my eyes, allowing the pleasure to wash through me as her loud screams and sharp exhales make me increase my speed. I'm almost there, but I want her to experience pleasure repeatedly. I push her knees back until they touch her shoulders.

"Oh my God, Mr Hayes, this is too intense," she mutters, squeezing her eyes shut and turning her head away. I know at this angle, I can get in deeper, and I know eventually, the pleasure will take over.

"I'm so fucking proud of how well you're doing, Angel and I know you can show me that you can take me anyway I give it to you, can't you?" She cries out as I push in.

"Ye-es," she stammers.

"Scream for me, Angel. Make everyone in this pub hear you scream and let them know who you belong to."

Chapter Thirteen

Angel

I push at Mr Hayes's stomach trying to push him away, although I make a half-arsed job of actually doing it. It's more like an automatic reaction every time he hits a certain spot inside of me. The feeling is all too much. It's not painful as such, but at this angle, it makes me feel like I'm going to piss myself, and I can't embarrass myself like that.

"Mr Hayes." He suddenly halts, slipping out of me, and rises on his knees, his penis bobbing, glistening with my juices, while I take exaggerated deep breaths to calm myself. The pressure I was feeling disappears immediately.

Mr Hayes stands and exits the room. Panic arises. I can feel my eyes stinging with tears. I thought I was doing well. He told me he was proud of me. What did I do wrong?

"Angel, stay right where you are!" he shouts, seemingly from my living room. *What is he doing?* I lay there, taking deep breaths. My pussy aches so much, but it's like he left me hanging; my body wants to let go again, and my clit still pulses for him. I pray he's not done with me yet. Shortly after, I hear the gentle sound of his footsteps on the laminate floor, and suddenly he's standing in front of me. However, what he's holding causes confusion to surge through me.

"Why do you have those?" I'm questioning and observing the lights for Macey's Christmas tree that he's holding. He approaches, with no words spoken.

Once again, he asks, "Do you trust me?" I give a nod while scrunching my face, still uncertain about his actions.

"You're so fucking perfect; now put your arms up for me, Angel," he whispers, before placing another soft kiss on my lips. As I raise my arms, he grasps one, encircling the lights around it, beginning at my bicep and continuing until he reaches my wrist. He's using Christmas lights to tie me up. *Oh, my God.* He takes hold of my other hand and encircles my other arm as well. I experience a constricting sensation as the wires wrap around me and I give a gentle pull on my hands, coming to the realisation that I cannot move. I crane my neck awkwardly and look up, noticing that he's attached the lights to my bedpost. He then crouches beside my bed, and I hear the click of a switch.

"I know you can take me, no matter how deep I go. Will you stay still and be a good angel for Daddy?"

I nod rapidly, whispering, "Yes, yes." He moves towards my door and flips the switch off so the Christmas lights provide the light in the room.

"My very own angel, waiting for me to do as I please." My heart races, frustrated by the limited visibility of Mr Hayes, but he climbs on the bed and leans closer. His eyes, filled with dark liquid, gaze longingly at me. The multicoloured lights are mirrored in his eyes. He positions my legs on his shoulders once again, but this time he puts both legs on his right shoulder. He doesn't give me any warning before he slams into me.

"Fuckkk," I scream. "Please, please," I plead, not really knowing what I'm pleading for. It's intense but also I don't want him to stop. He fucks me like he wants to imprint himself in me forever and at this moment I don't ever want him to not be inside me. He swiftly rekindles the building sensation with his punishing movements and the panic is back. *Fuck.* I don't know how to even describe the sensation. I want him to stop, but then again, I don't.

"Mr Hayes, please." I tug at my arms not even knowing what I would do with them if I got free from the tight binds, the cord of the lights constrict, yet the pinching sensation against my skin feels like a minor concern compared to the overwhelming urge to pee. "I…" *Oh my God.* "Please, I'm going to pee. Please." For some unknown reason, this causes him to increase his speed, and with no control, I am flooded with a peculiar euphoric sensation, shattering into pieces as it finally happens, and I soak Mr Hayes. My pussy squirts over and over. Everything becomes silent as the world fades away. I'm only aware of my heavy breathing and the pounding of my heart. It feels like waves of euphoria flooding over me, repeatedly, as if I'm intoxicated by every drug known to mankind. In the darkness, Mr Hayes shines brightly before me. His head drops down, his forehead touching mine as he thrusts twice more, my sensitive pussy feels his dick swell inside of me as his fingers sink into my hair and pull the strands while roaring out my name over and over. With each slower thrust, I feel Mr Hayes empty himself inside of me. He thrusts one more time, sinking so deep into me. My breaths blend with his, both laboured and intense. My soaking wet pussy flutters and my body continues to tremble beneath him, experiencing the aftershocks.

"Fuck, Angel. Fuck," he whispers, peppering kisses over my face which makes the butterflies in my stomach take flight. Mr Hayes sits up, still keeping himself buried inside of me. He looks down to where we are connected and his stare in locked with us as he pulls out of me slowly. The sting causes me to tense, but then I feel wetness trickle out of me and down towards my bum. Mr Hayes gulps and then runs his finger from the bottom of my arse up to my hole and pushes his fingers inside of me. Automatically, my back arches from the sting, but also from the need for him again. He removes his fingers as he glances up at me. "I don't think I'll ever be able to let go of you, Angel O'Sullivan." Closing my eyes, I am overcome with a sense of contentment like never before. I can't move a muscle, but being here makes me realise I can't let go of Mr Hayes either.

Chapter Fourteen

Angel

Boxing Day

The lack of warmth in this place makes most mornings quite chilly when I wake up. However, not today. As I open my eyes, I feel as if I'm trapped in a snug cocoon. Instead of a chill, there's only warmth in the air. I shift my position and sense the constriction that encloses me. I awaken, blinking my eyes and frowning as the bright light penetrates my window. I pivot inside the tight cocoon, coming face-to-face with a solid, hairy chest.

I tilt my head up, meeting his lazy gaze as he looks down at me. A small grin forms on his face. "Morning, beautiful." His raspy morning voice wakes the butterflies and they swarm my stomach.

"Good morning, Mr Hayes," I whisper, lowering my head to hide my morning breath. *Because come on, it's just a thing that we can't deny.*

"Tell me, how are you feeling this morning?" he asks, squeezing his arms tighter around me. I can't help but smile silly as I bury myself in his chest, surrounded by his masculine scent.

"Content, warm and happy," I muffle into his chest. I notice him pulling back a little, which causes me to furrow my brow. With a downward glance, his eyes flicker between mine and his lips tighten, showing a momentary hesitation on his face.

"Are you sore?" I give a shoulder shrug, feeling a slight ache, though I haven't moved enough to know for sure. I sense his nod as he places his chin on top of my head.

"I don't even remember falling asleep last night." I extract my arms from under the covers, revealing the faint marks that surround them. Confusion washes over me as I glance up at Mr Hayes. "Did you untie me?" His hands caress my arms in a gentle up and down motion.

"Yes, and I also did my best to clean you up with a wet flannel from your bathroom.

"What?" I manage to squeak. "What are you trying to say? You cleaned me?" My cheeks flush with heat as I hide my face deeper in his chest, anticipating his response.

In an effort to make me look up, he leans back and says, "Hey." I refuse, bringing the covers up and burying my head underneath them.

"Angel," he softly whispers. He lifts the covers and then lifts my face by placing his fingers under my chin. "Angel, what happened last night was the sexiest thing I've ever seen or heard." When his hooded eyes lock onto mine, things quickly become too hot to handle. I could never grow tired of this man.

"Do you know how fucking sexy it was to watch you squirt all over me? It's a moment I never want to forget." I quickly sit up and immediately regret my decision. My pussy feels bruised, even my upper thighs are sore.

"Ouch, ouch, damn." As I lie down again, the pain transforms into a dull ache.

"How?" I ask, looking at him as a feeling of horror consumes my body. I could feel myself soaking his dick, but I was too entangled in the amazing feeling it left me to question it. Until now.

Laughing softly, he gently untangles the knots in my hair with his fingers.

"I assure you, it's nothing to be embarrassed about. That's the sensation when you thought you were about to piss yourself. It was hot as fuck, Angel. I promise you." I nod, nuzzling myself into his chest, wincing as I rub my legs together, trying to make the ache go away.

"I assumed you might be feeling sore. I was a bit rough, I'm sorry, Angel."

My head shakes rapidly. "Don't you dare say sorry; I had one of the best nights of my life." I wince internally as I sit up and lean over to grab my phone. I light it up and see multiple missed calls from Mace and 38 WhatsApp messages.

"Fucking hell," I exhale as I open the chat.

Mace

Sounds like you weren't really sick, you lying hoe.

You sound like a demented cat.

Actually, your voice resembles a fox in a compromising situation.

Those screams are both tragic and dramatic; no man is that good, but A for effort.

What is mystery man actually doing to you in there? I have some concerns.

Wait, is this your V card that is being stolen away as we speak!?

I believe it is. Oh my God. Congrats, my baby.

Hey, where did my Christmas lights go?

I rub my eyes, then move on to rubbing my temples. I have no intention of reading the rest of the messages; they no doubt will get worse. Yeah, I know the walls are paper-thin upstairs, but did she have to listen in? Perhaps she could have turned on some music or something.

I raise myself to sit, taking deep breaths, as between my legs has an intense burning feeling. Right now, I feel like I'm sitting on burning coals.

"I have to go talk to Mace," I sigh.

"I think I should start heading out. I will probably have twenty-one questions from my family wondering where I disappeared off to," he says while stretching. I study his face, trying to find a sign that this will be our last encounter. He extends his hand and asks, "May I use your phone?" I give it to him, witnessing his fingers glide over the screen before a ringtone sounds from his trousers on the floor. "I have your number. I'll call you later?" he says, casually buttoning up his shirt. I give him a tight-lipped smile and stand.

"Fuck," I curse, my eyes welling up with tears.

"Grab ice and then take a relaxing hot bath," he suggests, putting on his top and picking up his trousers.

I nod abruptly, hoping he'll leave before witnessing my tears. Approaching me, he holds my face and tenderly plants a kiss on my lips. "Angel O'Sullivan, you're unforgettable," he murmurs against my mouth before his hands disappear from my cheeks. He cautiously looks out of my open bedroom door to make sure no one is about. Then he glances at me for a final time giving me a wink before disappearing. I find myself unable to look away from the door.

I quietly whisper to myself, "Goodbye, Mr Hayes." I really hope I get to see him again.

As I approach Mace's room, a headache starts to develop. I mentally prepare myself and open her bedroom door. "Here we go,"

She wears a sinister smile, like she can't wait to shred every single detail of last night out of me. Holding a coffee in one hand and a cigarette in the other—not that she is meant to be smoking up here, but rules are made to be broken, according to Mace—she motions with her head to a space beside her.

"There's a spot for you right here. Those are for you as well." She nods at the bedside table where painkillers and Sudocrem are waiting.

I frown, not understanding the reasons for the cream. "Sudocrem?"

"Well, by the sounds of you getting ragged out last night, I'm guessing the kitty is burning this morning." She rolls her eyes.

Ah, yes. With a sigh, I approach the bed, taking the coffee from her hand and gulping it down, acknowledging, "You're sick, but correct."

"You're so damn loud! What the hell was that last night and who was that guy?" she yells. "Furthermore, thanks for leaving me and the rest of the guys to run the place on our own. I think I have blisters from all the extra running around I did," she moans, wiggling her toes and frowning down at her feet.

In an attempt to evade her questions, I throw my head back against the headboard and release a groan. "Look, I'm exhausted. I feel like my fucking pussy lips are burning off as we speak. Help me." I stretch my arms in front of me and she grabs them, instantly examining the marks.

"What the fuck are these, Angel?" Her gaze swings to meet mine. "You kinky bitch, what did he use?" Her brows furrow as she tries to work it out.

"Well." I hesitate. "You know you were wondering where the Christmas tree lights—" Before I could even finish, a gasp leaves her mouth.

"I wondered why my tree looks like it has been ransacked." She gives me a disgusted look and curls her lip. "Keep them, you filthy bitch."

"Mace, you're a top hoe. Fucking help me. You must know what to do to stop this burn.

"Oh, you fucking wimp. Lay down on the floor."

Pointing at her, I firmly state, "My fanny is off-limits to you." She looks at me with disgust.

"I have no interest in getting close to your battered fanny, thank you." Rolling her eyes and shaking her head, she climbs out of bed and exits the room.

“Take this,” she declares when she comes back a few minutes later, passing me something covered in a tea towel. “It’s frozen peas. Lay on the floor and hold them to your fanny. It will soothe it.”

“Frozen peas?” I question.

“Yes, you fox, frozen peas. Trust me.” As soon as I lie down and place them on the outside of my shorts, I immediately experience relief. I’m also experiencing discomfort internally, which is probably normal, but I can't stop thinking about the candy cane.

“Mace,” I hesitantly utter, contemplating how to phrase this without triggering a barrage of questions.

With a roll to the side of her bed, she looks down at me and says, “Yo.”

“Have you, um, ever, you know?” I pause for a second. *How do I say this?* “Used food?” I suddenly blurt out.

“In English, please?” she sarcastically replies. I cover my face with my arm.

“In the bedroom,” I mumble. “Like using it while having sex?”

“Ew, no. What do you think I’m about to go down to the chippy and order a saveloy and make a night of it? What fucking kind of... Angel O'Sullivan? You didn't actually go there with a sausage, did you? Oh my God, was there even anyone in the room with you, you fucking freak,” she shouts. My hand falls and hits the floor with a slap.

"Shut the fuck up, Mace, no ew, fuck no!" I shout.

Her hand dramatically falls to her chest. "Thank God. Then why that question?"

Reluctantly, I side-eye her, knowing her reaction might differ when she hears how hot it was.

"He used a candy cane on me, or in me, should I say."

Her eyebrows shoot up and she gives a slow nod. "Okay, yeah, that's hot, but girl..." She props herself up, resting on her elbows. "That has UTI written all over it. Have fun." She smiles. *A fucking UTI.* However, I think having a UTI would be worth the candy cane fun with Mr Hayes.

Chapter Fifteen

Carter

New Year's Eve

As my eyes scan over the busy crowd in Westminster, filling the streets, I can feel the excitement building as they all prepare to welcome the New Year together. Angel and I have been in contact all week, and she told me that her and her friends got tickets to watch the New Year fireworks. As a result, I had to get tickets too. Thanks to Tyson's extensive contacts, I managed to score some last-minute ones, despite them being sold out for weeks.

Everything changed after that unforgettable night with Angel. She exceeded all expectations and then some. Although many people might assume it's only about sex, it's not. Although that's how I connected with her that night, Angel has always been intriguing to me. That's why I've been unable to stop watching her over the internet.

My encounter with her on Christmas Day left me feeling like a young man again. I had to face the reality that the girl I like will probably find someone her age and move on soon, but I can't fathom allowing that to happen. Now that I've tasted Angel O'Sullivan, I can't seem to get enough. She's a potent drug that has entered my bloodstream and won't go away. My eyes search the crowd and that's when I spot her.

My angel.

She shines brightly, like a beacon amid the crowd.

She messaged me an hour ago to tell me where they were standing to get the best view. She hasn't spotted me yet. I get my phone out to check the time; it's ten minutes until New Year, and the bustle and noise of the crowd shows everyone is excited for the countdown. One of the biggest attractions in London is the fireworks display. I've never watched them up close, but I'm unsure if I'll have the chance to see a single firework when she's nearby.

I type out a text.

I pull my baseball cap down, zip my jacket all the way up, and move closer to where she stands. Since it's crowded, I should be able to blend in without any problems. Yesterday, I sent Angel a small gift in the mail along with a note.

Wear me tomorrow night. – Mr H.

She followed up with a text, showing it out of the box, saying, 'Anything for you'. The intensity with which this girl aims to please me is mind-blowing, and I'm completely enamoured by it. I read about these lush toys and how you can control them from anywhere in the world. Every time she comes, I want to make sure I'm here to see her because I don't ever want to miss one. They're all mine.

Currently, Angel and I have one person standing between us, and I just need to find a way to get around him.

"Angel," I hear the guy shout. "Are you all set for the fireworks?" I can't see her in front of this lanky shit. From his voice, I can tell he's the jerk from the pub. To protect my identity, I retrieve my phone from my pocket once more.

Me

Lose the lanky shit. Now.

Roughly thirty seconds pass, and Angel enters my line of sight from the left side, still not looking in my direction.

Good girl.

I swiftly assume my position behind her, gripping my phone. I avoid touching her, so she remains unaware of my presence.

I activate the app I want and press the 'on' button.

"Fuck." Angel jumps in front of me.

"Are you okay?" Macey checks. Angel turns her head, revealing the side of her face, her lips slightly ajar, exhaling misty clouds into the cold air.

"Yeah." She nods before glancing up at the sky briefly. I raise the intensity by one level and observe her fidgeting.

"It's a chilly night tonight," I murmur. She freezes in front of me, quickly looks sideways, and checks to see if her friends are watching.

"Mr Hayes, what are you doing?" she whispers. The noise and commotion around us mask our conversation, but I have to lean in to catch what she's saying.

"I wanted to see the New Year with you, Angel." I turn the intensity up on the app which is connected to the toy she currently has inside of her. She lets out a low moan and tightly grasps my shirt as she reaches around her back with one hand.

"Mr Hayes," she moans. Looking skyward, she closes her eyes and takes deliberate deep breaths. She's an absolute vision, and I have a strong desire to bury myself deep inside her right here, right now.

Once more, I lean down and let my lips gently brush against her ear.

"I want you to remember this Christmas, Angel. I want to make you fall in love with Christmas because of me." As I increase the intensity again, her breathing quickens.

"Imagine the intense pleasure on your clit as my tongue savours your wetness. The feel of something inside you is my tongue entering you, drinking down everything you give me." Angel's legs must give out slightly as she falls into me and pulls on my shirt as her back trembles against my front. I bring my left hand up to her hip to keep her upright. Right now, if her friends looked, they would know she's in the midst of pleasure. With her cheeks flushed and her lips slightly parted, I have an overwhelming desire to taste and possess her.

"Mr Hayes," she mewls. "I'm going to—"

"Not yet. You wait until I say." The hurried nod she gives me causes a throbbing sensation in my dick.

I turn the intensity down as that lanky shit turns to her. I peep up from under my cap to see him smiling down at her. No one is watching her come except me.

She's fucking mine. Back off.

"Are you ready, Angel?" She remains silent.

"10."

As everyone starts counting down, I increase the intensity of the toy once again.

"Fuck." Her legs buckle and I embrace her, supporting her weight.

"I want you to know," I murmur in her ear, "you've made all my past Christmases pale in comparison. You brought a glow of light into my life. Angel, you are flawless, and I consider myself incredibly lucky to have you." Her moans grow louder, but the surrounding countdown screams overpower the sound.

"7."

"There's one thing you need to know, Angel O'Sullivan." I clench my jaw as she presses herself against me. "Your moans, sweet mewls, and kisses belong to me. Your sweet tasting cunt, tears, pain and heart are all mine. If you think another man will have them, think again. Good luck if you think you will get away from me because you, Angel O'Sullivan, have always belonged to me. You just didn't know. Mine!" I breathe out as I turn the intensity up to the highest setting.

"3...2."

Without caring about her friends' thoughts, she turns towards me, her emerald eyes shimmering through tears.

"Come for Daddy, Angel." Holding her by the waist, I witness her crumbling into shards. I shut off the device on my phone while she shakes against me, hiding her face in my chest. I lovingly run my fingers through her hair and lean in, kissing her. Her tears dampen my lips.

"Happy New Year, my sweet girl."

Chapter Sixteen

Angel

January

As I type on my laptop, a smile remains on my face while the words effortlessly pour out. I thought this story wouldn't happen or be good enough for the grade I needed, but ever since Christmas and New Year with Mr Hayes, I've been unable to stop writing. The short story was a minimum of 15,000 words, but I had already surpassed 28,000, and there was still so much more left to tell. I focused on editing it for the majority of last night. I think it has enough substance to become a complete novel.

And for the first time since I can remember, I love Christmas.

Or maybe I love Mr Hayes's of Christmas.

It's our first day returning to college. The deadline for our story is at the end of the week, but I was so engrossed in writing last night that I couldn't bring myself to sleep until I completed it. But when I woke up this morning, I had the idea to include more. I wrote the notes in a different

Word document because I couldn't add anything else to the current version due to the word count for our assignment.

While I wait for my classmates to settle after catching up with each other about what they did at Christmas, I keep my head down, hoping I don't have to engage in conversation. Normally I would be happy too, but I need to read over my work and make my final edits.

Mr Hayes sent me a text this morning, wishing me a good first day back and teasing a surprise later. The butterflies engulfed me as soon as I read it; of course, after everything we did, my mind instantly went to his dick, but we shall see later what he meant. All I know is when he's not around, I feel sick; like I'm anxious and something is missing, and then the minute he's around, or on the phone with me, I feel myself again. This is a completely new feeling for me.

My desire for Mr Hayes started when I first understood the feeling of wanting someone. Feeling like this is expected, given that no one has ever come close to him. I never anticipated these emotions to intensify so rapidly.

"Class," Mrs Finch says, walking into the classroom. "How was everyone's Christmas?" she asks cheerfully, clapping her hands and smiling at us. Mrs Finch isn't our normal English teacher; she teaches business, but maybe she's covering today. Everyone murmurs 'good' and 'it was great'

"We have a minor adjustment this New Year. Miss Cody has been moved to another college, but we have a new teacher joining us today." I let out a sigh and slump further into my chair. Miss Cody was great, and we connected really well.

My story is a bit out there. I won't describe in detail what Mr Hayes and I did because, well, this is toward my overall grade, and I don't know how my teacher would have felt if I wrote her a play-by-play of what some people may think is a disturbing porno. That being said, Miss Cody would have been okay with certain portions.

I followed her advice and expressed myself, just as she told me to. Damn it, I'll have to review it again and remove more content. I don't have the energy for this today.

"Your new teacher is incredible and has experience teaching at other schools. Although this is his first college, rest assured that his teaching and ideas are flawless, and I'm confident you will all get along splendidly." Mrs Finch is excessively excited, gushing more than necessary. Oh, but did I miss something? It's a man. Great. I have nothing against men, but I don't think they would enjoy reading a Christmas romance.

"Let's give a warm welcome to your new teacher, Mr Hayes." With a jolt, I turn my head towards the classroom door, and my eyes widen. Everything disappears around me except him.

There is no way; Carter Hayes is my new English teacher.

Oh fuck. Could this be the surprise he was referring to? While I'm freaking out inside, Mr Hayes enters the classroom with ease, flashing a smile that illuminates the room. As he approaches the front, his gaze doesn't meet mine, which makes me feel somewhat sad. Why am I not the first person he looks at when entering a room?

"Hi all." He gestures with nods throughout the classroom. Despite his lack of attention towards me, I'm now undecided about whether I want him to acknowledge me. My mum always told me that my face is a window to my emotions, and right now, it's displaying a thousand different feelings. "I'm Mr Hayes, your new teacher. Trust me, I'm laid back and encourage open communication," he says, a stern look softened by a small smirk. "As long as you behave like adults, you'll be treated as such." Mrs Finch, still grinning, stands by his side, and now I understand her excitement.

It would be wise for this woman to keep her married hands off my man.

My man, I think again. *Who am I?*

"I thought it would be a good idea to go around and introduce ourselves and maybe tell me the title of the short story you wrote. I am very excited to read each and every one." He smiles again, my insides melting slightly because he has a smile that will have any woman on her knees. It's evident that Mrs Finch shares my thoughts.

While he begins his rounds in the classroom, I'm a bit frustrated that my English teacher, who I lost my virginity to nine days ago, hasn't even glanced in my direction, leaving me in a state of internal turmoil. I understand it is intentional, but what is the reason behind it? Is he annoyed? Was he aware that I enrolled in this course? No, he did. I shared the news about the college with him. He had been aware the entire time and never even—

"It's nice to have you as my student again, Ms O'Sullivan."

Oh, you want to play it like that. Breaking through is the smile that has captured my heart, and his intense gaze, which I know all too well, overwhelms me as his once golden eyes transform into a deeper shade, as if visualising me in a vulnerable state, bound to my bed with the Christmas lights from Mace's tree. This thought is causing me to fidget in my chair. I'm tempted to respond flirtatiously, but I have to keep in mind that I'm in a classroom with other students and he's my teacher. It's unbelievable that he chose not to inform me. I respond with a sweet smile.

"Mr Hayes, I assure you, it's my pleasure." I blink twice innocently, appearing harmless. *If he wants to play, then let's play.* I am aware of how much he enjoys being addressed as Mr Hayes by me. "Your teaching is exceptional. You taught me everything I needed to know, so I look forward to the year ahead." I almost say *Daddy*, but I stop myself. Instead,

I release the word gradually from my mouth, with a slight drop in my voice. “Sir.”

With unbroken eye contact, I feel a sense of isolation from the rest of the world, as if it's just him and me, my heart pounding in my chest and an ache in my core, craving his presence. I crave every single inch of him; how am I meant to get through this school year, seeing him every day looking like the absolute snack he is?

How can I avoid imagining myself bent over the desk with Mr Hayes, brutally fucking me while addressing him as sir or daddy? I observe his nostrils widening as he inhales deeply. He adjusts his position to stand in front of the desk, crossing his legs and leaning back. Gripping the desk, he clenches it so tightly that his knuckles turn white, and his veins protrude on his arms. I'm too turned on to handle being around him for the rest of the day. Fuck. It seems like everyone is oblivious to the constant exchange happening within us. Slowly, I lick my lips as his gaze shifts from my eyes to my mouth. His expression shifts from a half-smile to a half-wince, followed by a raised eyebrow and a subtle nod towards me.

“Ms O'Sullivan, I am eagerly anticipating the year ahead as well. What is the title of your story?” I don a sweet smile, eagerly awaiting his reaction to the title.

“His Taste of Christmas, sir,” I add the ‘sir’ in, just to rub salt in the wound that bit more. Running his hand along the edge of the desk, he glances at it before turning his gaze to me. His eyes have transformed into a dark shade of brown, and his jaw is clenched.

"I look forward to reading it," he bluntly states before his attention returns to the class as people begin introducing themselves. I lower my chin and smile at the captivating story in front of me. Just one simple look and I can gather all the information I need.

He won't have me bent over that desk by the end of the year; he will have me bent over that desk by the end of the day.

The End? ... Naaa

Afterword

I hope you enjoyed my little spicy novella. Carter could have me annnnyyyyy day!

We all need to know if Carter gets Angel over that desk right? ;)

Join my Facebook reader group where I will share more on what's next for this couple.

PS. Black's Brokenly Beautiful Romance

Remember to leave a rating or review on Amazon or Goodreads, this helps us authors a lot :) Thank you x

Made in United States
Orlando, FL
25 November 2024

54484023R00083